THE FLIGHT
OF THE EARLS

Jerome Griffin

UPFRONT PUBLISHING
LEICESTERSHIRE

First Published 2002 by
UPFRONT PUBLISHING
Leicestershire

THE FLIGHT
OF THE EARLS

This is for my parents without whom,
for obvious reasons, I would not be here.

ACKNOWLEDGEMENTS

I would like to thank Upfront Publishing for embarking on this journey with me.

I would also like to thank Tony O'Brien for the wonderful cover; John Sheehan for the picture which makes me look vaguely normal – hasn't photography come a long way? Kirsty Sanders for her insight into the bizarre and twisted world of proofreading; Terry Lynch for casting his legal eagle eye over the contract; Martin Walsh – the best teacher who ever had the misfortune of having to deal with me – for introducing me to this episode in our nation's long and complex history; Donal MacMahon who demonstrated that this wonderful language does not rely entirely on Olivier accents; and other teachers who bore a positive influence on me – Tomás Begley, Bob Fitzgerald, Br. O'Connell, Bat McElligott and Paddy Bailey.

I must also acknowledge those who went before me and provided invaluable research material: *Tyrone's Rebellion* by Hiram Morgan, *The Great O'Neill* by Seán O'Fáolain and *Elizabeth's Irish Wars* by Cyril Falls.

I must also extend my thanks to 'The Clan' whose capacity for fun knows no bounds.

Finally, I must thank the two people who constantly endure my grumps and inane ramblings with minimal complaint – my mother-in-law, Baggins, and my wonderful wife, Joanne who possess never-ending patience and faith.

If I have missed anyone I'm very sorry, and I promise to make it up in the next one!

ABOUT THE AUTHOR

Jerome Griffin loves to write. He's very pleased that so many people love to read. Jerome lives in Buckinghamshire with his wife and mother-in-law – don't ask!

PREFACE

I fear I will never again set foot in this land – my land, my Ireland. What Fate sees fit to bestow upon me, I do not know, but in my heart I know I will never return. It's over, and because it's over, I have decided to set the record straight – to give an account of what really happened these past years.

History, they say, is written by the victors. Well, this is a history written by the defeated.

I am Hugh O'Neill and this is my story.

Contents

Chapter I
KIDNAP – 1587

A thick, grey fog hung low across the water as *The Matthew* pulled into Lough Swilley. It loomed up through the swirls of mist and glided ghost-like until it reached the docks where it took a well-earned rest. It hailed from Spain and had many fine wares aboard including all types of food and drink. Hugh Roe O'Donnell boarded the ship. He was oft named Red Hugh, not only to differentiate between us, but because his fiery temper was accompanied by a great flowing mop of flame red hair and these attributes were further exacerbated and enhanced by wild eyes with a manic glint, which suggested to the recipient of any prolonged stare that they should desist and yield forthwith lest harm befall them and their kith and kin. But on this particular evening, his spirits were more amiable. He was accompanied by Finóla MacDonnell, Fanad and na D'Túath MacSweeney, and one of O'Gallagher's sons, whose name escapes me. The group's aim was to sample the goods and possibly stock their stores with the Spanish fayre. Or just get drunk and have some fun, as is the wont of teenagers. As the evening fell into night, so it wore on into the early hours, yet the wine flowed and the senses dimmed. The drink overcame them one by one and when they were all a snoring like proper sailors, Captain Nicholas Barnes set sail and put to sea. Kidnapped and trapped like rats, Red and his cohorts could only despair at their predicament brought about by their own stupidity.

Hugh was incarcerated by the Lord Deputy – the English Crown's representative in Ireland – without charge against his good name, but *his* good name. At the time, this post was held by a spineless, devious and loathsome worm of a man called Perrot. Red's imprisonment, unjust as it was, was a masterstroke by Perrot. He had the vision to see what was happening in the north long before any of his contemporaries. He had the foresight to see that Red and myself were a huge threat together – even before we joined together – yet would be severely hampered by the other's absence. This is why he took the illegal action of kidnapping Red.

This was the straw that really crippled the camel. The injustices and crimes against the Irish as a people had been mounting for a good number of years but this act drove me to escalate my plans to gain emancipation from the English colonists. I was made aware of Red's kidnap the next morning and I was furious. Red's family, the O'Donnells and my own family had been enemies since the dawn of time, but I had met up with Red on several occasions in an effort to put the past firmly in place and move forward together united and strong. It had long been a failing of Gaelic families to fight independently of one another against the English colonists rather than combine forces in a show of strength. So Perrot must have worried at the prospect of myself, the Earl of Tyrone, and Red, the future Earl of Tir Connell, uniting in a common cause. Red and myself had made much progress and I needed him to organise and unite his ancestral domain of Tir Connell. I needed him to help me calm the waters between the O'Neills and the O'Donnells. I needed him to side with me in unity and demonstrate the strength of the Irish in the north. In short, without Red Hugh, I could not do it. So, it was a simple equation: I must have Red with me. Ergo, I must free Red.

I suspected that he would end up in the Tower of London, which would have been a disaster. As luck would have it, a few days later I was reliably informed that the far from salubrious dungeons of Dublin Castle had become his home for an indeterminate period. I immediately set the wheels in motion to gain his release – both in an official and unofficial capacity. While pleading with the Court to set him free or at least provide a valid reason for his imprisonment, I also oiled the hinges of the relevant doors at Dublin Castle through my contacts.

Eventually this latter approach began to pay dividends, but we would only be able to provide the first step on Red's rocky road home. We managed to tap the right people, either through bribery or blackmail, into opening the way for Red. It was up to him to seize the moment once it presented itself. However, even though it provided a good start for him, I suspected that it would be far from plain sailing after that. And I was proved right as Red related his tale to me.

★

'I had lost track of the calendar a long time before,' began Red. 'Occasionally, the gaoler would answer my questions and I would be able to keep count for a while. But in almost perpetual darkness, it is impossible to maintain accuracy. Sleep no longer follows a pattern and food is delivered sporadically or only at the gaoler's humour. The only gauge I could rely on to any degree at all was the temperature. In the summer, breathing becomes an almost impossible task. The stench of filth is further heightened by the searing, stifling heat. There are no windows and hence no breeze. They may be called dungeons but they do not sit below the castle.

'These dungeons offer no solace or warmth through the winter months. The damp freezes and the stone becomes ice. The only saving grace is the lack of wind and rain, and the only warmth is provided by your own beating heart. Many prisoners lose limbs through the frostbite as they languish without mercy, without hope. Others give up the game completely and await the skeletal spectre's icy clutch. I know not what drove me on – pride, determination, ambition, anger, hatred – maybe all of those and more besides. But I managed to survive until that night of the fifth winter of my own private hell when my cell was unlocked. I remember sitting there for a few moments thinking that my time had come and that this was but a dream and that what lay beyond the door was Death's own scythe waiting to reap his harvest. Eventually I summoned up the courage to crawl over to the dreaded portal and glanced out into the gloomy corridor. No scythe! But a faint flickering glow in the distance suggested the presence of a torch and so I made towards it. Whoever had opened my cell door had vanished. Once I reached the torch I paused a moment to get my bearings. On the wall fixing that held the torch was draped a rope. If my good Samaritan wished to remain anonymous, I decided it couldn't have been for any good reason. Time must have been against me and I would need to move fast if I were to make the best of this opportunity. I decided on my destination and set off towards the privy. Or at least towards what I thought was the privy. I crept slowly forward feeling my way along by the wall. Suddenly a movement to my right caught my attention just before a fist to my gut took all the wind out of me. Thankfully, I was hit by the fist first because I was also whacked over the back of my head by something weighty. But as the blow to my stomach made me bend forward, it reduced the impact to the back of my poll. As I fell there wincing in pain, I thought the game was up. However, before I had a chance to react, a foot was pressing my head hard to the floor as one of my attackers retrieved the fallen torch. I had deduced at this stage that there were two assailants. The one who grabbed the torch held it close to my face so that I could see nothing but its glow. It was that close that its smouldering smoke made me gag and I thought for a horrifying moment that he was going to push it into my face and blind me. I tried to struggle but my assailant's foot merely pressed even harder and suggested that a broken neck wasn't out of the question. I desisted my struggle and braced myself for the searing pain but it did not come. Instead, the fellow with the torch spoke.'

"'He's not the gaoler, Art!" he said. But he said it in Gaelic, I couldn't believe my luck!

"'Don't talk bullshit, Henry," replied the other. "In any case, it matters not. Let's kill him anyway."

"'No, no, no, don't kill me, friends!" I pleaded also in Gaelic.

"'He's speaking Gaelic!" said Art bewildered.

"'You feckin' eejit. Sure can't I hear for myself!" said Henry. "What's your name, lad?" he asked me.

"'Aaegh woo ownownal," says I. Actually I tried telling him who I was but my face was being pushed so hard against the ground that my reply was muffled beyond coherence.

"'Didn't catch that," said Henry shaking his head. "If he takes his foot off your head, do you promise to behave yourself?"

I tried to talk. I tried to nod. I could do neither.

"'I'll take that as a 'yes'," said Henry. "Art, take your foot off his head and put it on his back instead."

Art did so and I'm sure my insides have never been the same since.

"'Now, lad," said Henry again, "I asked you a question. What's your name?"

"'Aodh Rua O'Domhnaill," says I once more.

The foot on my back delivered a swift, sharp kick to my side and then reapplied itself ever more firmly.

"'Don't try to kid us, boy!" said Art and he exerted even more pressure.

'I thought he was going to squash me like a spider. I had become that weak and thin through five years of near starvation that I could do nothing to combat him. 'I'm not!' I gasped. 'I swear to you, I'm Red Hugh O'Donnell of Tir Connell.'

"'Well," said Henry, "he is supposedly in residence. I suppose it could be him. Now here's the thing, Red, if indeed you are Red Hugh O'Donnell, if we allow you to sit up, do you promise to behave yourself like a good lad?"

"'Yes," says I, feeling every breath being squeezed from me. I could have cursed myself for giving in to their mocking manner, but at the time I felt I had little choice.

"'You had better not try anything," said Henry, "or you will end up wearing an ugly reminder of this torch all the days of your life."

"'I promise," says I through gritted teeth agreeing reluctantly.

"'Okay, Art, let him up."

'His cohort grudgingly obliged and I sat up with my back to the wall. Henry held the torch very close to my face, mainly because its light was a little dim and he wanted to get a good look at me and see if I was who I said I was, but also so I didn't go getting any ideas for myself.

"'Fiery, red hair. I'd say those are O'Donnell eyes," he said. "I can also see in those eyes that he would love nothing better than to gouge out our insides, Art, and eat them in front of our very eyes. Yes, I'd say he's O'Donnell all right."

"'If that's the case," said Art, "we should kill the prick anyway."

"'Hmm," replied Henry in deep thought, "you may be right,

Art. But if we stop to think for a moment, we can put a proper perspective on the whole situation.

"'What do you mean?" said Art getting heated. "He's a feckin' O'Donnell, Henry. Do you not remember what his people mean to ours?"

"'Aye," replied Henry, "I do. But it strikes me as a little funny that we are all free to do as we please in the corridors of the dungeons of Dublin Castle."

'Henry paused and, in the gloom, I could sense that he was looking back and forth between myself and Art.

"'Now I'll give ye something to think about, lads," continued Henry. "It is obvious that someone has engineered our escape. However, I can't help but think that if they truly wanted us to succeed they surely would not have released an O'Donnell with a couple of the sons of Shane O'Neill. I'm Henry, by the way," he said extending his hand to shake as if suddenly remembering his manners, "and this is my brother, Art."

I took his hand and then his brother's.

"'I had deduced as much," I said to Henry, "to be honest with you."

"'Aye," said Henry, "they did say you were quick on the uptake. So, young Red Hugh, do you see where I'm coming from in my thinking?"

"'I do," says I.

"'Go on then," he said.

"'Well, I would imagine that influential members of both our families have tried both the official and unofficial routes to securing our freedom. It would appear that the unofficial route has succeeded, hence our situation here and now. However, there is a factor in all of this, which I cannot identify, that has thrown us together."

"'My thoughts exactly," said Henry. "And what do you make of the situation?" he asked me.

"'Well," I began, "I think they are looking for us to kill each other, or more to the point, as there are two of ye and just the one of me, they are hoping that ye kill me."

"'Maybe that's just your young ego talking, maybe not," replied Henry. "But I'm certainly thinking along the same lines and I also think that – just for this once mind – that we should join forces."

"'What?" bellowed Art.

"'Calm yourself, brother," soothed Henry. "Just think for a moment. They want us to kill each other. Well, I am refusing to help the Sassenachs kill their enemies. At this moment in time, an enemy of the English is a friend of mine. When we arrive home in Ulster, we can sort out our differences. Until then I'd say we have a better chance of getting out of this hell alive if we work together. What do you say, O'Donnell?"

"'I agree completely. Much as it galls me to work with the sons of Shane O'Neill, I'd rather do anything than help the English. And I'm hungry for revenge against these bastards."

"'Good," replied Henry, "Art?"

"'I suppose so," said his brother after a moment's thought.

"'Okay then," said Henry. "Where is the best place to go to try to get out of here?"

"'The privy," says I. "We just float out in the sewer. Far from pleasant I'd imagine, but you O'Neills should be used to it."

"'Don't push your luck, O'Donnell!" said Henry. "I see the sense in working together but I can easily change my mind. However, you are probably right to say that we should escape through the privy. Now where is it?"

"'Well, I'm pretty sure I was heading in the right direction before I got clobbered," says I.

"'What makes you so sure?" asked Henry.

"'Just a vague memory of when I was brought here the first time. I'm sure that this downward slope leads to the privy, which makes sense if they are to dump it in the moat."

"'Fair enough," replied Henry. "It's not a lot to go on but it's all we have got. So let's make tracks and let's try to keep the noise to a minimum – no talking!"

'We moved on in virtual silence guided at the head by Henry with the faintly glowing torch. I was in the middle, with Art bringing up the rear. All that could be heard was the occasional scuttle of a rat – every dungeon prisoner's companion – and every now and again as we passed a cell, we could just make out a fellow prisoner's groan, sniff or sob: all sounds of despair. I ached to free them or help them in some fashion but I had not the means. And I'm sure that both Art and Henry felt the same. However, even if we could free them, it would mean swelling our number too much which would surely court danger. And we could ill afford any other obstacles besides our hunger and ragged, near naked, appearance in the bitter winter cold. We moved on slowly in the narrow, dingy and, above all, dark corridors, and soon I felt the walls closing in. I began to experience trouble breathing and it was all I could do just to keep moving forward. I was beginning to panic and was liable to crack under this strain of the mind when I became acutely aware of another sound. It was the sound of rain outside. More than that it was the unmistakable sound of rain lashing on a body of water. The moat! Surely we must be nearly there. It was then that I realised that there had been another deafening noise all along and I only noticed its presence after it was gone. It was the pounding of my heart. It was a wonder the O'Neills didn't ask me to keep it in control. But we were nearly there now and no mistake, and that's all that mattered. My spirits lifted and I began to calm down. The corridor eventually led to a flight of stairs, which took us down further into the bowels of this cesspit. And I'm not kidding, it was certainly the bowels. We knew without a shadow of a doubt that we had nearly reached our quarry. The stench was evil itself and it made me believe that all of mankind's effluence came through this point. At the bottom of the steps the corridor widened into a room which was to all intents and purposes the dungeon's sewer.

'I could see that the O'Neills were in as bad a state as I, for they were continually wiping tears from their eyes and gagging. To gag was all we could do: the rotten excuse for food we had consumed hours earlier had long gone and there was nothing there to bring up. But to actually vomit would have been heaven for it would have left a better taste and odour. Instead, as we gagged, each deep breath brought another lungful of that rancid air into our bodies and forced us to gag again. Eventually, Henry forced himself to speak.

'"Let's just find the fucking opening and get it over with," he eventually managed to say between retches.

'Myself and Art could only nod and we groped our way

around that hellhole searching for the opening. It was easier to find than we anticipated even in the pitch dark. The ground and the walls sloped and channelled the shit down through a chute, which puked it into the castle's moat. So the three of us trying to move cagily forward were slipping and sliding in the shit until we hit the wall. There we managed to secure the rope to a long disused manacle iron and dropped it out of the chute. From the feel of the iron it was rusted worse than Guinevere's chastity belt and we were unsure as to whether it would take our weight. But we had no choice. It was decided that I should be the first to descend, as I was the lightest. Of course I was afraid because what we were attempting was unknown. It was dark. We could not see. We didn't know how far the drop was. We didn't know what it dropped on to. We didn't know if the rope was long enough. All we knew was that I would find out first. I made my way down the rope hand over hand and soon my arms felt as though they were going to explode. Searing hot aching pain throbbed in my muscles, but I knew I had to keep going. It wasn't long before I reached the end of the rope and I decided to look down for the first time. To my joy I could see the moonlight reflected on the water of the moat. It was then and only then that I noticed the putrid stench of the stagnant water. Still, it was a huge improvement on my previous environment. I let go of the rope and as I fell towards the rancid water, I gave a thought to its depth. As I broke the surface I gasped in panic and managed to take in a lungful of the foul liquid. Thankfully the moat was quite deep so there was no real harm done. As I came back up to the surface from my hellish plunge, I puked up the evil, slimy fluid, and once my coughing and gagging and spluttering came to an end, I called up to Henry and Art that all was fine.

'Henry followed almost immediately, and as I pulled myself on to the bank from the ice cold water, Art also descended the rope. Unfortunately, Art was substantially heavier than either Henry or myself and the iron manacle gave up the ghost and collapsed under his weight. In his unplanned drop, he toppled and spun in the air and he crashed into the castle wall. Myself and Henry immediately dived back into the near frozen moat and rescued a now unconscious Art. I'm a good swimmer but the big man's dead weight frame was too much for me and so it was Henry who really saved his brother from drowning. Henry, as you can imagine, was utterly exhausted from his exertions and he lay gasping on the bank while I tried to revive Art. After a few minutes Art came round coughing up much more of that foul water than I ever did. It's almost bizarre and perverse but I pitied him more for that than I did for his crashing fall. He complained of pains to his head and his right ankle, which on closer inspection proved to be cut and swollen respectively. We weren't too worried about his head, as he seemed alert enough – for Art, that is – but he could put no weight on his ankle. This turn of events would alter our plans significantly.

'We were just discussing what we were going to do, when we became aware of some rustling in the bushes. Discretion being the better part of valour, we decided to hide and observe. Soon enough the figure of a man could be seen stealing through the scrubby shrubbery looking towards the castle. We remained absolutely still and once again I felt that my heart would give us away with its thunderous beat. Then something caught the man's attention and he stopped and stared at the castle wall. I looked around to see what he was staring at. It was the rope! In our panic to save Art we had contrived to put all our lives in danger by ignoring the rope, which had managed to get caught somehow and still dangled from the chute. In retrospect, if the manacle had stood firm we would have been in the same predicament anyway, so it was no matter. I was beginning to think that we had not put a lot of thought into our escape plan. At that moment I think we all feared for our lives. Through our sparse cover we could see him move towards the bank to inspect the rope closer.

'Henry signalled to both myself and Art to be quiet. He then signalled that he would make his way around to the right while I was to move a touch to the left. The man was walking almost directly towards us and we knew that Art could not move of his own accord and that to help him would obviously draw attention to ourselves. So instead, Henry wanted to use the element of surprise and outflank him. As I crawled through the reeds and brush, I clutched at my chest to stop my heart from breaking through my very skin. I stopped when I thought I was the same distance from the moat as my target. Slowly I raised my head so that I might spy him. Suddenly, a voice called out in a harsh whisper and I ducked my head in fear and panic. I lay there motionless for a moment fearing that I had been spotted and my life would be ended by a bullet or a sword, or even worse, I would be thrown back into that living hell of a cell. And then it registered. I think the first thing was the Gaelic floating into my mind. But then I realised what the Gaelic had said: "Red Hugh O'Donnell, where are you? I am Rory O'Hagan and I am here to offer assistance."

'I looked up again and realised that it was indeed Rory O'Hagan, and Henry seemed to realise this at the same time for he leapt up and made himself known to Rory. He had brought some food and water, and as we ate he explained how the bribes within the castle had been brought to bear by yourself, Hugh.'

I nodded to Red only too glad to be of help and insisted he continue the story of his escape.

'However, it became clear that Art and Henry were not part of the plan and I could see Henry's mind working overtime. Art, on the other hand, couldn't find his arse with both hands and a compass, and so he sat quietly eating. Soon enough we came to talk of our next step in our adventure together. Henry played a cagey hand, knowing he could not look after his big ape of a brother on his own. But the last thing he wanted to do was go with O'Hagan and myself. At the end of the day, I am an O'Donnell and O'Hagan is your ally, Hugh, and you have the power to make life very uncomfortable for your cousins, bearing in mind that their father killed your father. Eventually he made up some cock and bull about getting help from relatives in Wexford and that he would go to them. He also noted that Rory had brought provisions enough for two and now they were stretched already. Rory and myself tried to persuade him against this course of action because we had made a gentlemen's agreement and we would honour it. But I could see he didn't trust us. I can't say I blame him. I'm not sure what I would have done had our roles been reversed. However, we would take his brother to the home of Fiach MacHugh

O'Byrne across the Wicklow Mountains. I think Henry believed we would take care of Art because of his injury, but in the future when they were both fit, he believed we would turn on them. To be honest I was far too thankful for their help, courage and companionship in the short time we had spent together to even consider harming or wronging either of them. However, we delayed saying our goodbyes until after we had made it out of Dublin and were safely away from the throng. Even though Henry was right as far as the provisions were concerned, we gave him some food to help him on his way. Then he headed south to Wexford and we went west to the Wicklow Mountains.

'The bitter cold weather made it a particularly harsh journey in our scant and threadbare clothes and soon we had also run out of food. The meagre provisions that Rory had brought were for two people over a few days. Our number, as I have already said, was doubled and the length of the journey was easily tripled by our immobility because of Art's injury. We radically reduced our rations to cope in the hope that we might come across the odd rabbit or pheasant in the mountains. But sure we might as well have hoped to find gold at the end of a rainbow, as the weather was that hard and unyielding. A vicious wind constantly swirled around us, stinging our ever more frail bodies. When it wasn't raining it was hailing, and eventually as we ascended higher, and higher it snowed incessantly. Not a berry could be found on a tree and not an animal ventured out of its hibernate winter home. Art tried with all his might not to hold us back but sure his leg was damaged badly and without time and rest for it to heal, it just grew steadily worse. We were reduced to a crawling pace after a couple of days when we reached the summit of our mountain. To our eternal horror we discovered that we were not where we thought we would be. The snow had covered everything and the sky was that dark that we could only use the sun as a vague guide and we had ultimately got lost. Art O'Neill in his hunger, fatigue and agony – I felt his leg was probably gangrenous – was delirious and could go no further. He insisted we go on without him but that was never an option. Besides, I was also nearing my last ounces of energy and would soon be unable to continue. We needed to proceed due south but that way was a deep and dangerous ravine. We would never last by going around it as it would take too long and we were in no fit state to tackle it. All I could think of was the biting cold. Rory practically dragged myself and Art over the summit and found a small ledge, which would provide a little shelter. It was the best he could find and so Art and myself lay and waited while Rory continued south to Fiach MacHugh O'Byrne to get help. As I watched Rory disappear into the snowstorm, I wept and repeated over and over, "Cold, cold, cold, cold, cold…" Nothing else was in my thoughts.

'And that was the last thing I remember until the pain as my sparse clothes which had frozen solid on to my body were torn from my skin in the efforts of my rescuers lifting me from my icy bed. I could hardly see. As I tried to focus, I could just make out vague dark shapes against the bright white snow. They were carrying me on some type of stretcher and they covered me with animal hides. I fell unconscious again.

'It's very strange, for the next few days I drifted in and out of consciousness in my delirious state. It was apparently touch and go whether I would survive or not. All I remember about those days is extremes of sensations: the warmth of the bed; the cold, clammy sweat of the fever; the wholesome aroma of broth; the comforting crackle of a fire in the hearth; the smell of burning turf, and the screaming pain of amputation. The frostbite took both of my big toes as spoils of victory of a battle in our war, which I eventually won. Let it have them. I get more use out of my sticks than I ever did out of those toes. Anyway, I'll not blame the frostbite; I'll blame the English. And I'll use it to stoke the fire of revenge.

'As you know, Art O'Neill lost more than his toes – he lost his life. So in many respects, I got off lightly.

'Anyway, Hugh, the rest of the story is known by you. With your help I was smuggled back to Tir Connell and now my father is resigning the chieftainship to me. I owe you my life and my wife. I completely agree with you that this feud between our families must stop and I am resolved to help you to end it.'

★

And so Red married my daughter and we worked together to unite the clans. It was remarkable. No, it was more than that: it was a miracle. In but a couple of years the feud was all but forgotten and the O'Neills and the O'Donnells lived side by side in harmony. Well, maybe harmony is stretching it a touch. Let's call it living cordially.

My aims, however, went far beyond uniting our families. I wanted to unite the whole of Ireland. But this is a delicate business to undertake. It must be conducted surreptitiously so that the English do not see the bonds forming. For years they had relied on their policy of divide and conquer which was such a huge success across the globe and paid great dividends everywhere they went, especially Ireland. And with so many loose tongues about the country, I needed to tread carefully as I tied the knots. Because of this, my progress was painfully and necessarily slow. Through marriage, trade, fostering and other methods, I gradually built up special relationships with many of the northern clans and I encouraged all of them to do the same. Even though this was a time-consuming task, which required patience and understanding from all parties, within a few short years I had built up a strong network of reliable clans.

Not strong enough, though, that I would trust any of them with the full knowledge of my plans – not even Red. I must confess that I was pondering how to make them ready for such a challenge, when a bizarre twist of fate lent me a helping hand.

Chapter II
CONSPIRACY AND CONFEDERACY – 1592

Years of corruption, abuse and maladministration had led to bitter resentment and widespread discontent among the Irish people, and something needed to be done. Red, of course, was eager to wreak a bit of havoc after the suffering he endured at the hands of the English. Maguire also liked to indulge in a touch of *rúaile búaile* and I knew of others who had good reason to take some action. However, I was truly surprised at the number of lords who also held the English in contempt and sought vengeance. I had no doubt that there was a sizeable support for change but I had no idea the majority was so huge. Also, the feelings of revolt did not stop there and the support among the masses was incredible. I had long since believed that I could ignite the flame of rebellion enough to achieve my ends but I had no idea that the flame was already lit and billowing furiously. Sure, everybody grumbled, but that is just human nature. It is almost an unwritten rule that the monarchy and government must be despised in equal measure and all laws and taxes deemed unfair, but the average person has an enormous capacity to adapt. No matter what the Queen decides, it seems, two reactions will follow – first the public will bemoan its lot and then they will get used to the change and take it for granted. And soon enough the changes fade in memory and the situation will always have been the same.

Well, it appears to my incredibly good fortune that the Irish people have longer memories than I had anticipated. They remember all the injustices and suffering, all the pain and abuse, and all the unfair changes through the years. And they have nurtured a powerful passion for vengeance.

So, when I learned through my spies that Red was launching a secret confederacy of Gaelic lords, I was, of course, intrigued and very interested. No doubt the neglect in seeking my support was a fear of my English connections and loyalties. Of course they were not to know that I secretly harboured plans for rebellion. But they would soon. I decided to pay a visit to Red and have a wee chat – unannounced, of course.

'Hugh!' greeted Red in shock and surprise giving me a big bear hug.

'How goes it, Red?' I asked.

'Fine, fine,' he replied. 'The wife never said you were coming.'

'Oh, I never told her,' I said, leaving it hanging in the air like an executioner's axe.

'Then, should I have been expecting you?' he asked in a perplexed manner.

'No, no,' I said nonchalantly.

'Oh, I see,' said Red. 'Then to what do we owe this pleasure?' he asked.

'No reason, no reason,' bland as you like. 'I just fancied visiting. It's not awkward, is it?' I asked in a concerned tone.

'No, no,' he replied too quickly, almost cursing himself in the process. 'Actually, that's not quite true,' he added. 'It's just that we have company arriving tonight and sure we have no room for you to stay.'

'No room?' I replied in amazement. 'Why it must be some gathering in a place this size that you can find no room for your father-in-law.'

'Yes, there are a great number staying... it's a bit of a celebration...'

And I could see in his face that he wanted to drag every last syllable of his poor excuse back down his throat. 'A celebration?' I asked with raised eyebrows.

'Yes.'

'I'll have to be sure and flog Jamesie when I return home, for I received no invitation.'

'Well, no, you see...' and again the face hinted at a mistake.

'Ah, I see,' I said as his eyes dropped to his feet. 'You did say you were not expecting me, ergo, no invitation.'

'Well, you see, Hugh, I can explain...'

I was really beginning to enjoy watching him squirm.

'Go on then,' I said.

Silence.

'Well?' I demanded.

'You see…' he began.

'I have plenty of time, Red,' I said. 'I can wait for you to fabricate another tale for my benefit.'

He just glared at me.

'I don't have to invite you to every function I host,' he snarled.

'True, true,' I conceded. 'However, as I am already here, I might as well stay.'

He glared again.

'It's all right,' I said. 'I'll keep out of the way and will not cause you any embarrassment.'

'You can't stay, Hugh,' he replied almost apologetically.

'Why not?' I asked perplexed.

'Because you will not like the company,' he said by way of explanation.

'Really?' I replied and left my response hanging once more filling the hall with emptiness. Red, as I had hoped, felt a need to fill it.

'It's going to be rowdy and raucous and not at all an atmosphere which will please your more sophisticated sensibilities.' He was beginning to allow his lie to run out of control.

'A party then! Why if you truly believe, Red, that I don't enjoy the *craic* at a good old-fashioned Celtic gathering, then you do not know me. I would be only too delighted to stay and have some fun. Now then, where am I going to sleep?' I asked as innocently as I could.

'No!' he bellowed almost losing control completely. 'You cannot stay, Hugh. We are gathering for a specific purpose and you will not find the subject palatable.'

'On the contrary, Red, I think you will find I possess a voracious appetite for bloodthirsty rebellion, but I can just hide it better than you and the others.'

This revelation took the wind out of his sails entirely and he remained slack-jawed and speechless. So I continued the conversation.

'You look shocked, my dear boy. But cheer up, for I am truly here to join your party, not spoil it. But if we are to form this confederacy, then we must do it properly. We just cannot afford security leaks like the one, which allowed me the knowledge of this meeting. God knows if Fitzwilliam or Bagenal or one of the other shites knew about this gathering, it would already spell the end for all. We must be cute and clever and do things slowly. Now before the others begin to arrive, why don't you take me through your plans as they stand and see if we can analyse their strengths and weaknesses.'

And so Red outlined the grand conspiracy in its most basic form.

'I think it has merit but it is too ambitious too soon. And it lacks for one vital ingredient,' I said.

'The sea,' replied Red knowingly.

'The sea,' I concurred nodding.

We both knew that we could strike victory after victory on the land but it would all be useless if we could not keep the English from our shores. They possessed the strongest navy the world had ever seen, while we had none. We desperately needed to rectify this situation before we even raised a musket in anger.

'We have thought about this and truly do not know how to solve the problem. They will always have that advantage over us.'

'Not necessarily,' I replied.

'How? What would you suggest?' asked Red.

'Spain!'

'But that is merely a matter of swapping masters! It will make us no better off.'

'That, my dear son-in-law, depends entirely on how we play it,' I replied.

'Well, how would you suggest we "play it"?' he asked sarcastically.

'Slowly, cautiously, religiously and confidently,' I replied.

'You've lost me, Hugh,' replied Red.

'Okay, in its most simple form, we begin our rebellion slowly and cautiously – the last thing we want to do is enrage the English enough for them to crush us in one fell swoop. We just want to do enough to irritate them and alert others abroad. We will steadily escalate our rebellion and progressively court Spain. We will use religion as our common ground and we will present ourselves as equals so that conquest is never an option and servitude is not on the agenda – merely religious brothers united against a common enemy.'

However, even though I reassured Red with these words, I had secretly often wondered and worried about our future with the Spanish should we succeed and bring about this eventuality. We know the English have been cruel, deceitful, greedy, arrogant bullies, but would we fare any better under Iberian masters should that become the situation? I sometimes think we should maybe adopt the old proverb, 'better the devil you know than the angel you don't', as a motto. When all is said and done, all the available evidence suggests the Spanish may be even more ruthless than the English. Especially when we consider the Inquisition and the Spanish colonies in the Americas. However, I don't know why but I feel that our future would certainly be brighter under Spanish rule. I sincerely hope that my faith in them is not misguided.

'If I had a tendency towards cynicism,' began Red smiling, 'I would suggest that you had put some serious thought into this campaign even before you knew it was going to happen.'

I matched his smile with one of my own as I replied. 'Sure, cynicism is not necessarily a bad thing in a man, Red.'

We laughed as we shook hands and then Red retreated to an almost sombre tone.

'We will encounter problems this night,' he said. 'Hugh Maguire is set to be one of the main players in our confederacy and he is not best pleased with you since Belleek.'

At Belleek earlier in 1592, I had served with Marshal Henry Bagenal, my brother-in-law, for the crown forces as we put down a rebellion instigated by my other son-in-law, Hugh Maguire. I had never seen eye to eye with Bagenal or his father, Nicholas. I courted and eloped with Henry's sister, Mabel, in an effort to bring the families closer and create an alliance with them. But my action only served to fuel their hatred of me, and so I resigned myself to the fact that we would always be enemies, even when we fought together for Elizabeth against my son-in-law. I did not want to fight Maguire, but I was put in an impossible situation. Prior to the revolt I had made personal pleas to Maguire to refrain from his actions and bide his time which would surely come. I could not tell him of my own plans for fear that they would become widespread knowledge and I was far from ready to engage in any conflict at the time. But Maguire had been wronged harshly as Captain Willis had been sent by Bingham to sheriff Maguire's lands. Naturally, he wanted justice, and when that failed to materialise, he sought vengeance. I failed to persuade him from his course of action and I was forced once again to display my loyalty to the Crown by stamping on the rebellion as it sought to blossom. However, I swore an oath then that it would be the last time I would serve the Crown against my fellow countrymen. I had served against Desmond in Munster in 1584 and now against Maguire and it made me sick to the pit of my stomach. I had had enough and so I escalated my training programme, strengthened my defences and injected speed into my preparations. The next time I would be ready.

'Worry not about Maguire,' I said to Red by way of reply. 'I knew he and many of his sympathisers were coming and that they hold no love for me or my kin.'

'Is there anything you do not know?' he asked in wonder.

'Well, as far as this night is concerned I believe I am adequately informed. Also, just for gossip's sake, I have heard that Burghley prefers boys. And I think I am right in saying that this morning Her Misery – which I believe is Maguire's pet name for the Queen – had bread, cheese and ham for breakfast.'

'Hah! You even know our private jokes! But I can't believe what you say about her breakfast!'

'Well, it is Wednesday,' I replied drolly.

'Fair enough,' shrugged Red grinning. 'Is that true about Burghley, by the way?'

'So rumour has it.'

'Well, I'll be buggered!' said Red.

'No, that's Burghley you are thinking of!' I replied.

Red laughed and shook his head.

'I will not even pretend to know how you got your information,' he said, 'but how do you intend to appease

Maguire?'

'Oh, I have my ways,' I replied.

'I don't doubt that for a second,' he said. 'But for now, let's eat and then prepare for the other guests.'

I could see that I was the recipient of many a wary glance as the other parties trickled in through the late afternoon and early evening. Conversations struck up throughout the hall as old friends caught up with each other and I mingled accordingly doing the same. But I would have been a fool to believe that I was truly welcome. However, I was just biding my time and waiting for Maguire to arrive, which no doubt, was what everybody else in the castle was also waiting for. Red was busy playing the genial host and was the epitome of calm and control, or at least, if he was nervous, he did not show it.

And then it was time. Maguire and his entourage entered the hall and launched into their own catch-up. But the news of their arrival wafted through the room like a bad smell and within seconds the cacophonous drone of myriad conversations petered out and came to a halt.

'What ails ye?' bellowed a bewildered Maguire.

I walked to the centre of the hall so that he could see me.

'What is that bastard doing here?' he demanded of Red.

'He has come to join us,' replied Red.

'He has in his hole,' retorted Maguire. 'If anything, he has come to spy on us for his lord and master.'

'I assure you I have not,' I said. 'My allegiance is to Ireland.'

'My bollocks it is!' said Maguire. 'Where was your allegiance but a few months ago when you helped them defeat me at Belleek and make me a refugee in my own land?'

'I tried to warn you of your actions, Maguire, but like always, you refused to listen. Did I not tell you it was a mistake to rebel at that time? Did I not tell you to wait and see what would happen? Did I not tell you that you would realise a better opportunity? But you had to do things your way and look what happened.'

'If you had sided with us then we would have seized victory. But it's too late for that now. I'll have your black heart on a platter this night, O'Neill!'

'You will not!' bellowed Red. 'Not in my house! Just calm yourself, Maguire, and hear what the man has to say.'

'I refuse to listen to a traitorous liar out to feather his own nest. And you, Red! I'm surprised at you letting this yellow-livered Sassenach lover into your house.'

'Ach, Maguire, cop yourself on, man!' replied Red. 'We are all out to feather our own nests – except O'Neill. Just hear him out and then decide upon your course of action. But there will be no killing under my roof.'

And so I took the floor. And you could have heard a flea breathe as I outlined my plans. I told them of my preparations thus far: my stock of munitions, my weapons, my army, the training, the fortifications, the communications and spy networks, everything. I analysed our strengths and weaknesses and our needs if we were to gain success. I talked of the Spaniards, the Italians, the French and the Scots who were all willing to help. I told them of the English: the dangers we faced, the threats they posed, the advantages they held, their powerful soldiers and leaders. I demonstrated where previous Irish rebellions had faltered and exposed the cracks in the English set-up. And when I was finished there was silence. A silence, that enabled me to savour the moment. I had harboured so many grievances for so long in silence that I smiled as the weight of my confessions liberated my mind for the first time in my life. I sighed and opened my eyes. I had not realised that I had closed them. And I saw the faces of many men deep in thought. The silence continued unabated and not one of us felt the need to fill it, for everything had been said. And at that moment I knew that they had accepted me, even Maguire who had tears welling in his otherwise hard, cold eyes. I gazed about me and noticed that not one of these many men were looking at me, at each other or at anything in particular. The focus of their attention dwelt not in this world but deep in their minds' eyes. It would have been more appropriate for the trance to be broken by a crash of thunder or a flash of lightning, but it wasn't to be. And so 'twas my walk to the table to fill my glass with wine which distracted their thoughts.

One or two people began to move and whisper words to each other. And soon enough the hall was buzzing once more. Red and myself were joined by Maguire who offered his hand to me and so I shook it.

'Powerful speech, O'Neill,' he said. 'You have obviously thought this through in great detail.'

'I have contemplated nothing else for twenty years and little else before that. But now I feel confident that we can actually achieve victory.'

Both men raised eyebrows at this revelation and I continued with my confession.

'I have been living parallel existences for some years now and nobody really knows who I am. 'Tis my greatest weapon and I intend to use it to telling effect.' I told them things I had never shared with anyone else and they listened intently only nodding or shaking their heads from time to time.

Chapter III
MY FRIEND, ALONSO

It was soon after this that I met a man who would become one of my dearest friends and one of my most devoted brothers-in-arms. Alonso Cobos was sent by the Prince of Asturias to meet up with me and investigate our position so that the prince might decide whether helping our cause was a viable option. We managed to strike up a rapport almost immediately, which helped put my mind at ease. It is incredible how enterprises as important as ours could quite conceivably live or die on the humour of one person or the relationship between two people. If Alonso had been another man, our revolution might never have happened if he thought it unworthy. However, from the moment Alonso met myself and my generals, there was never any doubt that he would not recommend assistance. He was an incredibly likeable gentleman and his amiable nature was highly infectious.

I took him through my plans, strengths and weaknesses, and likewise on the enemy's side. There was but one sticking point.

'I have had this map made by one of the best cartographers in the world. He used the most up to date, modern charts and it clearly shows the advantage the geography gives us,' I said to Alonso. 'As you can see, the River Bann, Lough Neagh and the River Blackwater provide superb natural boundaries to the east and south. The River Erne practically joins the Blackwater also at the south, and coupled with the Shannon effectively separate Connaught from the rest of the country. At the same time the rugged coastline provides but a few landing opportunities.

This means that there are relatively few entry points into Ulster – namely the forts at Enniskillen and the Blackwater, and also O'Connor Sligo's castle in Sligo. Apart from that, on the boundaries there is Bagenal's stronghold at Newry and a couple of garrisons in Armagh and Monaghan. Access to the heart of the province is also hindered by dense forest, mountains, streams, tributaries and bogs. It really is not an ideal place to attack. I intend to make it our fortress.'

'You say that the coastline bears few landing points, but surely the English can access the rivers virtually unopposed as they have the best navy the world has ever seen and you have... well, you have none.'

'Aye, that is very true. But the rivers still leave them on the outskirts and will not suit their battle plans. For them to succeed, they must draw us out from Ulster and defeat us on their terms. Only then will they be able to successfully invade our lands and quell any rebellion as it dies before them anyway.'

'So how do you propose to defeat them? If your plan is purely defensive, how can you possibly drive the English from Ireland and claim her for your own?'

'We will start small and clever. We will lay siege to their garrisons and starve them into submission. Should a relief column arrive, I am convinced that we will secure victory on the battlefield. My spies will keep me informed of their movements every step of the way so that we remain always prepared. News of our victories will spread far and wide, and soon all of Ireland will join us in revolt. Our Catholic struggle will be cheered and encouraged by our Catholic brothers in arms across the continent. And we will gain the assistance of his majesty King Philip II of Spain. When and only when all of Ireland has joined us and we have the support of Spain, especially the navy, will we attack the English and bring final and total victory and freedom to these shores.'

Chapter IV
TIME TO STRIKE – 1594

Due to myriad factors, my life has always seemed to conform to a game of politics and balancing acts. Each and every time I have managed to deal with a given situation, another would poke its head up and demand a similar level of attention and delicate planning. Maybe this is true for each and every one of us and it is merely this puzzle called life. I don't know, but it seemed that where I preferred to devote a deal of thought to a problem before making a move, more often than not my immediate colleagues would be champing at the bit to take action through a veil of red mist and in the heat of the moment. Because of this I felt almost compelled to play a political game with them in an effort to restore control. It was always a balancing act with an emphasis on time.

After the meeting of the confederacy in 1592, we took no real action for nearly two years, save for the odd raid on English landlords. I knew that many of my contemporaries were restless and thirsted for blood but I was unwilling to strike a blow until we had the full support of Spain. They were certainly interested and considered us a useful potential ally in their war against Elizabeth. But as yet they had not committed wholly to our cause and I was anxious to receive a guarantee of sorts before I lifted a finger towards the road to war. However, I also needed to be realistic. The Spaniards could hardly commit to a rebellion that did not exist. We needed to make a gesture of sorts, at the very least to convince them.

So, eventually I conceded to myself that we needed to strike our first real blow. But how? How could we deliver a meaningful victory over Elizabeth that would gain the assistance of Philip and not incur the full wrath of the Crown in the process? This was my dilemma. I puzzled over it for weeks. How could it be done?

It could not be done. But it must be done. So how? How?

And then it hit me. It was on a beautiful summer's morning without a cloud in the sky and a wafting gentle breeze for a fan in the sweltering heat. I was out riding on my own along the banks of the Bann when it dawned on me that our objectives were simple on their own but apparently difficult together. So I broke down the separate elements and solved them. First of all we had to strike and secure a victory – simple enough. All I needed to do was ensure that we held all the advantages. Secondly, it was imperative to ensure that Elizabeth did not counter-strike immediately. Again this was simple enough. We just had to strike in the late summer and inflict a defeat that was neither crushing nor too embarrassing. Third on the list was securing the assistance of Spain. So we had to launch a rebellion and gain a victory – that's all they wanted, a gesture. And finally, it was essential to avoid incurring the full wrath of the Crown. This was the element that caused me most concern and the one that had the most obvious solution. All we had to do was maintain the appearance of the balance of power. If Elizabeth thought she had as many friends in the north as enemies, she would rest at ease. So it was imperative that I publicly appeared outraged at our victory and protest my undying loyalty immediately. I smiled to myself as I returned home, and on my return I discovered that I had a visitor – Red. A very anxious, angry and agitated Red. He, as did all the other confederates, wanted to strike and was frustrated by my stalling. Well, now I was ready to strike but I was not about to let anyone know that. I would strike but I would do it with a great deal of reluctance.

Sometimes it is difficult in retrospect to believe that we ever managed to agree on anything. Red and myself had such different attitudes to everything. We were two different peas from two different pods entirely.

We had been arguing for months about the best course of action to take. Red, with his fire and passion and enthusiasm and belief that we could rally the whole of Ireland to our cause in an instant, was intent on storming Enniskillen and then driving on to destroy Bingham. As I have said, I favoured a more cautious and patient approach.

'Hugh,' said Red as he stood in front of my desk, 'I cannot raise the numbers we need on my own. I need you to support this confederacy in the open. For the sake of all that is sacred, you are the O'Neill in all but name. You have the power. You have the position. And the most important of all is that you have the support of the people. Now let's use it, man!'

'Red,' said I in response rising from my seat, 'I admire your passion – you know I do. But passion without caution and guidance will see us all swinging from the traitors' gallows.'

'The hangman holds no fear for me!' he ranted. 'Let them call me traitor! I care not. I'll never serve or submit to that whore as long as I live!'

'Red, that's just the point! We are traitors in the technical sense of the word at the very least. And I know that neither of us will ever bow to her again. But we gain nothing and lose everything if we act rashly. Together we have strength and we have the support of some very influential people. But if we behave like outlaws or even present Elizabeth with an opportunity to label us as such, then our support will disappear before the English even raise a bow in anger.'

'Then we will fight our own battles!' responded Red walking around the desk arrogantly. 'I would never have put you down as a coward, Hugh, but your talk is flecked with yellow.'

At this point we were standing nose to nose glaring at one another.

'Red,' I said meeting his steely stare with the epitome of calm and control, 'I understand that you are upset and angry—'

'Angry?' he blasted. 'Jesus Christ, Hugh, you're picking up their knack of understating every issue, man! We have taken insult upon insult and harm upon harm. Back in '86 my own father, Hugh Dubh, drove that bastard Willis into the sea when he tried to invade and take our home. My father had had enough back then and that was eight years ago! Have you forgotten what they have done since, let alone before then? Have you forgotten how they stole O'Connor Sligo's castle from him? Has it slipped your mind that Bingham drove O'Rourke from his Leitrim home? That Fitzwilliam hanged MacMahon and took his lands? And now this atrocity on your own son-in-law Maguire. That bastard

Willis has got his foot in the door of Fermanagh and you wish to sit idle. Let me tell you, Hugh, it won't be long before they are knocking on the door of Dungannon at this rate.'

'I know what they have done, Red, and what it means to all of us. I also know it is just the latest in a long list of crimes against our people. But see sense, man! They could crush us in an instant. If we do things your way, we gain vengeance and possibly a token victory. Then we swing from the gallows and our families lose everything. If we do things my way, we gain a nibble of vengeance, a certain victory and the chance to hit them again. We lose nothing. It also buys us time, and believe me, time will become our most valuable commodity.'

I paused for a moment and thought.

'I wasn't going to tell you this until I had more definite news,' I said. 'However, I feel that now is the right time but you must swear that it will go no further than your ears.'

Red looked at me suspiciously at first and then nodded. 'I swear,' he said.

'Good. As you know, I am presently courting King Phillip II of Spain for assistance in our struggle to come. I am also corresponding with King James VI of Scotland, but I think our best chances lie with the Spaniards. Between our two clans we have full control of Ulster, but we must strengthen our defences first. However, what you don't know is that my aims and plans moved beyond Ulster quite some time ago. We can secure victory in all of Ireland. I'm certain of it. But it will be a slow process. It cannot happen overnight. We need to slowly convince the Irish people that we can gain ultimate victory over the English. We need to get beyond our petty differences and clan bickering and become one strong nation. And we must have foreign support to achieve it.'

I paused briefly to allow this to sink in. 'However,' I continued, 'I do believe you are right when you say that only the two of us can rally enough support. You are also correct when you say that something must be done now. So, here's what I propose: you and Maguire go and lay siege to Enniskillen. It is important that I am seen to be loyal to Elizabeth, otherwise it will seem as though the whole of Ulster is in rebellion and they will send an army to crush us. If they feel they have an ally in me, it will put their minds at rest and they will not be so anxious to get here. So I will condemn the action publicly. I'll also send Art and Cormac in a couple of weeks with a few hundred bonachts for reinforcements. They will, no doubt, in time send a relief column to Enniskillen. You must destroy this and Enniskillen will fall. The English, believing they have a friend in the north in me, will sit out the winter and wait for spring to seek revenge. In the meantime, we will spend the winter replenishing stocks, gathering the harvest and fortifying Ulster.'

'I see nothing wrong with that,' replied Red.

'So, we are agreed then?' I asked.

'Yes,' said Red. 'I'll go and make ready.'

'Good. Before you do, Red, I'd like to offer a word of advice.'

'Go on.'

'I know you are bitter towards the English after what they did to you, but keep your head up there. The longer we remain alive, the more revenge we can reap.'

'Right,' he said grinning, 'I'll bear it in mind,' he continued as he turned to leave.

'Oh, and Red?' I said.

'Yes,' he responded turning once more.

'You ever call me a coward again and you won't need to wait for the traitors' hangman to make a widow of my daughter.'

He stared at me for a moment, nodded and left without another word.

Chapter V
THE CHAPERONE

Red had given me his word that he would not act rashly, but I am an extremely cautious fellow and I believe fervently in investing in a little insurance. So I summoned my brother Cormac for a meeting.

'Cormac,' I said to him, 'I want you to take three hundred foot and one hundred horse and go to Red and help him in his siege of Enniskillen. However, the military strength you will take is a bit of a smokescreen. I have an ulterior motive for sending you to Red. I want you to keep him out of trouble – be the eyes in the back of his head, the guardian angel who banishes his devil, the friend who makes him see sense. He is strong and wilful and may get carried away and want to do something stupid. Don't let him do it.'

'That's easy for you to say, Hugh!' raged Cormac incredulously. 'But putting it into practice is a different kettle of fish altogether. You just said yourself that he is strong and wilful. If he decides to go off on some foolish adventure, he is more than capable of convincing all to follow. And how do you propose I stop him?'

'By convincing everyone else, not to go with him before he gets a chance to sow the seeds of any foolhardy plans. You will have a few days before the relief column arrives. Convince Maguire and the others to keep to the plan in the way we have rehearsed. Repeat the message over and over until they are convinced that there is no other way. Try and ensure that Red doesn't get fully involved in the battle. Drive the issue from the start. Our aim here is not to beat the English in open battle – that's *their* game. They are the best at it and they would make light work of us. Our aim is to inflict defeat on the English in our territory and to make their strongholds here unmanageable.'

Chapter VI
BISCUITS

It was an awful experience knowing that my dearest friends and family were to be engaged in a battle many miles away and I was unable to help them further. I had done all I could to prepare them for the siege and the ambush, but not being there myself meant that my impact on proceedings was limited to advice before the event. Not being able to influence the event itself was a situation I did not relish and one I never wanted to experience again. But it was essential that I distanced myself from proceedings for the time being. The English believe in their policy of divide and conquer, and achieving a balance of power in their colonies which renders opposition to their rule virtually useless. So it was imperative that I publicly condemned the action and vowed to bring the perpetrators to justice if I were to convince the English that they still maintained that balance of power. That way, if all went according to plan, by the time the English realised that I was against them, their line of communications on the Ulster border would be in shreds and the province would be our fortress. We would be prepared.

However, even though I was supposedly publicly opposed to the siege and unaware of developments at Enniskillen, I managed to keep a close eye on the situation. I just could not help myself. I was supposed to wait for official news to break and then receive a report from Red when it was all over, but I was too anxious, so I had someone keep me up to date daily. So when Red arrived at Dungannon to deliver his report, he would have known that I had received official news but not an in-depth insight into proceedings, so I played dumb and allowed his eloquence to flower.

'Cormac your brother and Maguire headed south to Drumane by the Arney stream,' said Red, 'to intercept the English relief force led by Sir Henry Duke and Sir Edward Herbert. The enemy had no more than fifty horse but their strength was almost one thousand men. Of course I include the churls in this number. There were maybe seven hundred soldiers maximum. They were carrying a hefty quantity of provisions – food, clothing, powder, shot – enough to keep the garrison going for two months, I'd say.'

'Did they get any of it through?' I interrupted, apparently eager to know everything.

'Settle down, Hugh,' said Red laughing, 'and hear my account in its entirety. Now then, where was I? Oh yes. So Maguire and Cormac had taken one thousand men to meet them while the rest of us continued the siege. So all we could do was wait.'

'Whose idea was it for Cormac and Maguire to head south?' I asked.

'Cormac came up with that plan and it was masterful,' said Red. 'His idea was that it would tire the English out before the main battle.'

I looked at Cormac and he shot a smile, which suggested that he had achieved his objective of keeping Red safe. I smiled back.

'Of course,' said Cormac butting in, 'we were not planning on engaging in an open battle. We were merely going to harass them and sap their energy before they reached Red at Enniskillen.'

'That's right,' said Maguire, 'and also to prevent them from laying waste the land as they had been doing on their march north this far.'

'Right,' said Red. 'May I continue with the account now?' he asked the other two tetchily.

'Sorry, Red,' replied Maguire. 'But sure I'm only excited by our victory. Go on with your story.'

'Fine so,' replied Red. 'Well, I was waiting with my men ready for the real battle to arrive and all we could hear for two hours off in the distance was the sound of sporadic fighting as the lads engaged and drew off before the enemy could get a hold of them. Of course, the English needed to concentrate on marching to Enniskillen and protecting the supplies as well as fighting off their attackers. Sure they were completely shagged by the time we had a sight of them. They had suffered some casualties from their harassed march, which slowed them down even further as they collected and carried their injured and dead. However, their slow pace virtually halted altogether when Cormac and Maguire drew off completely and the fighting stopped. There then descended an eerie silence, which lasted for a few minutes as the English drew breath. "I wonder," says I to my brother, Rory, at this point, "do you think the bastards know what awaits them here?"

"'I doubt it," he says to me, and I think he was right. I'm sure that Duke and Herbert thought they had seen off our feeble resistance as we would be too frightened to get caught between the garrison and themselves. I'm sure they must have thought that Maguire and Cormac's force represented the entire siege and that the rest of their march would be worry free.

'I gave the order for our horse to attack. We weren't close enough to see their faces but their physical reaction suggested that they weren't expecting this turn of events. Our horse whirled in and out and disrupted the enemy's order as little pockets of their men gave chase. And these were then isolated as Cormac and Maguire returned to the fray immediately and picked them off at their will. I then ordered ranks of musketeers to fire shot after shot into the enemy's van, which was breaking up before our eyes. The English fought back bravely and Duke and Herbert at first unbelievably attempted to continue on to Enniskillen. However, I believe they must have assessed our numbers quickly and soon gave the order to retreat. They abandoned all the supplies and beat a hasty exit from the battlefield and, I must say that Duke and Herbert did very well to close their ranks and save their force from utter destruction. They were truly routed and I feel they will not recover too quickly from the sting inflicted upon them at Béal Átha na in Briosgadh (The Mouth of the Ford of the Biscuits).'

'Biscuits?' I asked.

'Yes,' replied Red. 'So called because of all the food – primarily biscuits – which was abandoned by the enemy and lay scattered all about the battlefield and floating in the river. This was meant for the relief of Enniskillen, and when the men saw it, they knew that the castle would fall.'

'And what of the pursuit?' I asked Red.

'We did not give chase, Hugh,' replied Red.

'Why not?' I cried. 'Surely they were there for the taking! They were on foot and slowed down by their dead and wounded. What possessed you not to get after them and deliver an even greater victory?'

'Well, initially we did, but with all the best will in the world, Hugh, the men were tired after a hard-fought battle.'

'Well, I would suggest that the enemy was even more exhausted!' I retorted.

'What would you have us do, O'Neill?' interjected Maguire. 'The victory was good enough and the men wished to enjoy the spoils. We ordered a pursuit but it was only attempted half-heartedly and so we drew off so we could enjoy our glory.'

'Glory? I barked. 'If we don't drive home our advantage when we have it, there will not be much in the way of glory in the future. I have a letter here from a very reliable source, which suggests that Duke and Herbert considered themselves extremely fortunate to escape at all let alone with three quarters of their force. We must have discipline if we are to succeed, gentlemen. It's that simple. Rest assured, had the outcome of the battle been reversed, Duke and Herbert would have seen to it that not one of you lived to tell the tale. *We* must be as ruthless.'

There was widespread silence. I had dampened their spirits and quenched their joy. I knew it was a great victory but I also knew it could have been far greater.

'In a tree full of bees' nests we have destroyed but one,' I said. 'When we have the opportunity, we must ensure that all those bees are accounted for. And if any escape, it must be our will, which allows them to escape so that they have a harrowing tale to tell. We cannot allow them off the hook so easily. Especially right now. The fact that the nest was not completely destroyed means that it still poses a threat.'

I allowed this to sink in before I continued.

'You did very well, gentlemen. I do not mean to be harsh. You followed our training methods through to fruition and you showed discipline and courage in equal measure. It was only at the end that you faltered. And, even then, it was just a matter of allowing yourselves to be human. But, alas, we cannot afford that luxury. We must not allow compassion to invade our hearts – not for the enemy and certainly not for our men. Our advantages will be few and far between and we must capitalise on them when they materialise. It is a lesson we must learn quickly.'

Chapter VII

INTO THE LION'S DEN

A few days after the battle of the Ford of the Biscuits, I called Red, Maguire and my brothers for an impromptu meeting at Dungannon. I explained that even though the year was too far gone for the English to raise another army for the north before winter set in, they would surely attack early in the spring. And all the while the sting of the Biscuits would fester as they waited. So I had decided to take pre-emptive action.

'And so I must go to Dublin and soothe the council,' I said.

'Have you completely lost your senses, man?' yelled Maguire. 'You will be arrested for sure. There is no way you can feasibly believe that you can just march into the lion's den, have a wee chat and march right back out again.'

'But it is exactly what I intend to do,' I replied.

'Well, we will not allow it to happen,' said Red in a very matter-of-fact manner. 'We will not let you go because we cannot afford to lose you, Hugh. If the success of our campaign depends on any one individual, then that individual is *you*. Your people need you here. Let the council scream all they like for an explanation and a submission. You will not venture out of the safety of Ulster.'

'I have been left with no choice, Red,' I replied. 'I don't mean to harp on about it, but the fact that we never took advantage of the situation presented to us at the Ford of the Biscuits means that the enemy can still pose an extremely serious and dangerous threat. They would need but a few reinforcements to be able to mount an attack on Ulster before the winter sets in. While I remain confident that we would defeat them on our soil, I believe that it would be, at the very least, extremely damaging and, at the worst, ultimately disastrous. Given time we can turn Ulster into an impenetrable fortress, but she is vulnerable at the moment.

Also, the last thing the men will want right now is to engage in a bitter battle with a hardened enemy seeking revenge. There is a harvest to be gathered and that must be our priority. I must go to Dublin and buy some time.'

'If you go to Dublin, Hugh,' said Maguire, 'you will end up rotting the rest of your days away in the dungeons of the castle, mark my words.'

'I think you underestimate my diplomatic skills, my dear son-in-law. I will go to Dublin and profess my innocence and undying loyalty to the Crown. You forget that I have already publicly condemned the action of the Ford of the Biscuits. I will then promise to bring the rebellious scum to heel. That's you, by the way, gentlemen,' I added, which received a chuckle. 'I will be hailed a hero and then I will return to Ulster and we will build our fortress.'

'You have truly lost your mind!' retorted Maguire. 'I do not doubt your diplomatic skills at all, Hugh, but I just refuse to believe that even you can convince the yellow-livered fools this time. I fear for your safety.'

'Worry not, Hugh,' I soothed. 'In but a few short weeks time we will laugh about this as we prepare for Christmas.'

'I hope you are right,' said Maguire resigning himself to defeat in this argument.

'I still say we cannot afford to allow you to go,' said Red.

'We cannot afford to not allow me to go,' I responded. 'Do you not see, Red? If I refuse to cooperate now, we will be forced into an unwanted fight we are ill prepared for. It is better that I should go and calm the waters at least until their opportunity to attack us is passed.'

'I see your logic,' replied Red, 'I just think it is flawed. And besides, if we must fight, we will fight. I think we are more ready than you know.'

'Red, we have already secured a physical victory on the battlefield. Now let us strike a mental victory at court. The English will not know what has hit them if we start winning the political battles as well. Trust me, I would not go to Dublin if I feared for my safety. I am certain that I will return. And I know I must go. It's our only option.'

'Well, it seems your mind is made up. I still don't like it, though,' grumbled Red.

'I feel the same as Red,' said Maguire, 'but your confidence has convinced me. However, I cannot help feeling that you haven't told us everything or perhaps there is something we have missed.'

'Aye,' said Red, 'that feeling has been nagging away at me as well.'

'Well, worry not,' I replied. 'Everything will work out just grand.'

As the council broke up and I watched Red and Maguire walk away a little disgruntled, I could see why they felt it was a poor move. And yes, I was withholding some information from them. But I had just cause. I did truly believe in my own persuasive abilities and I was convinced that I could secure the time and terms we needed to build our defences during the winter and continue our campaign come the spring. However, my confidence was not all down to my ability. I was not about to take a huge gamble like this and risk throwing away all those years of careful planning. I had also put in place an insurance plan. Let's just say that the majority of the Dublin Council were 'grateful' for my existence and could little afford for the reasons of their gratitude to become public knowledge.

And so I went to Dublin. And I answered the charges. And I denied the same. I swore allegiance to Elizabeth and promised to bring peace once more to the province. I also pledged my sons as hostages and the sons of other chiefs. And at the end of proceedings, seven of the thirteen council members were satisfied that I was a good and loyal servant, and so we reached agreement. I would return to the north and maintain the balance of power. Of course, it would have served them more harm than good to do otherwise. Over time they had each benefited from my existence in a number of fashions and at the same time I could, if pushed, have provided Her Majesty with information on each of these magnificent seven individuals which she might find unsavoury, to say the least. No, they had no option but to say that I was a thoroughly nice chap and let me return home to the north to go about my business. Of course, I had no intention of honouring any of the terms of the agreement. They had broken many a promise prior to this. I intended to serve them a portion of their own medicine and watch as they were forced to swallow the bitter bile.

I could hardly wait to get home to find out how this news was received.

Obviously, Red, Maguire and all of the others were delighted and astounded that I had managed to achieve all that I set out to achieve. They did not know that it simply boiled down to a matter of bribery and blackmail. And they did not need to know.

It is just a matter of exploiting weaknesses. And there are not many weaknesses more vulnerable than the purse and honour. I would, of course, tell them in my own good time, but for now I needed the rumours of my cunning victory in Dublin to spread and grow. Our fellow countrymen, the common English soldiers, and, most important of all, Spain, needed to know that I was capable of succeeding in this struggle. It gave me a great sense of satisfaction knowing that my endeavours were, at this minute, being relayed, embellished and exaggerated far and wide.

This was just another example of a game I played quite frequently. I enjoyed toying with the minds of people just to see how they would react. It also served to make an enigma of me. At one point a few years previous I bought a quantity of lead in England with the excuse that its purpose was to mend the roof of my castle. As soon as I got the lead home, I had it melted down into bullets. Why, you may ask, would I go to such lengths if I could simply acquire bullets from Spain, France or Scotland? And the answer is simple: it gave the men a boost. They would relay the story to comrades by the flickering light of campfires on cold winter evenings and chuckle at the thought of us getting one over on the enemy. Over time the story would take on legendary proportions and become exaggerated beyond all recognition as I single-handedly smuggled my lethal contraband out from under the nose of Elizabeth. The more these stories were generated and embellished, the more vulnerable the enemy became in the eyes of my troops. And this was absolutely essential. It was imperative that I reduced this great English Army to weak human beings before a battle of real significance took place. We needed to be ready. And this victory of the mind at Court carved another chink out of the metaphorical English armour. I was pleased with the way the news was received by the men.

However, I must admit that, from a selfish point of view, I gained more satisfaction from hearing of the reaction of Bagenal and Elizabeth. I was told that all of Bagenal's blood rushed to his head giving the impression of a giant tomato and threatened to burst his skull apart. He raged and threw tantrums for days. He beat his servants to vent his anger and frustration. He swore oaths of revenge and bemoaned his lot to the world at large.

Elizabeth was equally livid yet less demonstrative. The council were labelled incompetent buffoons to a man and their reputations lay in shreds. The truce secured in Dublin was certainly seen by the English as a more embarrassing episode than the Ford of the Biscuits.

I was content. We had secured two significant victories and had the time to get our house in order. I was determined to inject an even greater sense of unity into the clans and to ensure that Ulster was impenetrable come the spring. There was no time to rest. We had work to do.

Chapter VIII
FORTRESS ULSTER – 1595

The Battle of the Ford of the Biscuits had brought us a valuable victory. Our discipline was outstanding, our patience immaculate and our plan unblemished. Even Red maintained perfect control and made Cormac's job very easy indeed.

However, Red calling me a coward struck a nerve deep within me and forced me to open my eyes and ears more towards our people. I never dreamed in a million years that Red actually believed I was yellow. But it was evident that someone did. I decided to dig for the truth and see how attitudes towards me lay amongst my people. I soon discovered that there was an element that doubted my courage and application and that this element was winning over some support. At the moment it was a minority but I would need to take action to quench their spark. All too often minorities are dismissed as insignificant and of no consequence. However, I believe that a crowd of two or three hundred can cause serious damage once united. It was, in my opinion, a dangerous situation.

By this time we were well into autumn and everyone was concentrating on gathering the harvest. Knowing we had a truce in place was but a minor comfort. If the English decided to break the truce as they had done on numerous occasions in the past, then we would need to be ready. But I knew we would not have to worry too much as the English would not be in a position to seek revenge for the Battle of the Ford of the Biscuits until the following spring, so I decided to take a more active role in supervising our defences. Throughout autumn and winter we trained our troops and fortified the province. As we had done for some time, our own officers' ranks were swelled with Spanish officers and English deserters. We also employed the same tactics and trained one group of men to battle readiness, stood them down, and trained another group so that we never exceeded our quota of allowed forces. Any English information would hopefully relay stories of an available force far smaller than our real strength. We also trained peasants which had never before happened in an Irish Army. This was the cause of much distaste among many of my peers but I cared not. They proved to be as good a soldier as any gentleman and helped to boost our numbers.

I also travelled the province overseeing defensive works on our homesteads and lands. The natural barriers of rivers, mountains, forests and lakes which helped cordon Ulster off from the enemy, were reinforced by the plashing and counter plashing of all the routes into the north. This entailed weaving the woods together branch by branch. Our men worked on this so thoroughly that it would take the English months to try and cut through any passage. Especially as they would wait until spring when the growth would be even more dense and tangled. I found my inspection of the defensive work at the boundaries was an incredibly rewarding experience as we could really see for the first time a unity in the people, which was never there before. There was also an overwhelming feeling that they were protected from invasion by the English. I didn't fully share their enthusiasm on this front just yet. We were certainly in a better position than ever before without question, but there was a long way to go yet.

My actions during the autumn and winter went a long way to regaining the confidence of many doubters, but it did not deliver entirely. For that I would need to go the distance. I decided that when spring came and hostilities resumed, as they inevitably would, I would complete my betrayal to the crown and take direct action against the forces of oppression.

Once Ulster was secure, Connaught would prove to be an easy task because of the beautiful yet awesome Shannon. The river is the longest in the British Isles and comes but a few miles short of severing Connaught and Clare from the rest of the country.

Those few miles would need to be reinforced defensively, and once that relatively simple task is accomplished, it would render the north and west of the country practically impenetrable and a virtual fortress. In fact, I began referring to our secure lands as,

'Our Fortress', which quickly caught on and soon the men were using the term freely as they grew relaxed and comfortable in their new safety net.

As long as we could maintain our defences, increase our numbers and continue to strike blows against the English, the greater our chances of securing Spanish aid. We could then strive to liberate Munster and make inroads into Leinster. With reinforcements from Spain, we could then make our final drive into the Pale and Dublin as our final target. I dreamed that it would be almost fitting if the ultimate showdown took place at Clontarf where in 1014 Brian Boru defeated and banished the Vikings from Ireland. Only this time, with the help of Spain and the determination of the Irish, we would ensure that the invaders would never return.

Chapter IX

INCURRING THE WRATH

As 1595 marched on, it became clear that the English were feeling a little insecure and vulnerable. I think they were beginning to realise that their line of communication across south Ulster was a little weak and the source of many easy targets. Their concern was further heightened by the difficulty in revictualling the forts because of the distance between the forts themselves and also the distance to any port or food stocks. The infrequency of the deliveries of supplies and the general scarcity and poor quality of food was also leading to extremely low morale, chronic living conditions, illness and desertion. Indeed, desertion numbers, it was said, would have been dramatically higher but for disease.

In May that year, my brother-in-law Sir Henry Bagenal, attempted to do something about this state of affairs. He managed to gather together a force of about two thousand, which included fifteen hundred soldiers, the rest being kerne and churls. He then embarked from Newry in an effort to revictual the Blackwater Fort. My spies, as ever, provided a fantastic service and relayed the information to me that very same day. Fortunately, Red and Maguire were with me when I received the news.

'I think that we should prepare a little welcome party for my dear brother-in-law,' I said.

'I was thinking along the same lines,' grinned Red.

'Yes, it's about time we got back in action,' said Maguire. 'I've been hungry for this moment since the Biscuits. When and where do you think we should prepare for battle?'

'Both of you go an make ready your armies. Myself and my brothers will meet you at Clontibret,' I replied.

'You're taking part?' asked Maguire shocked.

'Yes,' I replied evenly. 'It's time the English learned exactly what level of force we have at our disposal.'

Silence greeted this initially. Then Red was the first to speak.

'What about not incurring the full wrath of the Crown?' he demanded. 'What about not showing our full hand? What about appearing to maintain the balance of power in Ulster?'

'I always said that we would need to maintain that pretence until the time was right. Well, I now feel the time is right,' I said.

'Hugh,' said Art, my brother, 'I'm not doubting your judgement or anything, but the Spaniards have hardly demonstrated complete support, let alone delivered anything of note, yet. Do you not feel this action is a bit hasty?'

'No, I don't think so,' I replied. I didn't want to show our full hand until Ulster was sufficiently defended and now I think it is. We have spent the whole winter making it so. I also feel confident that we can secure a resounding victory to add to the Biscuits which will make, not just the Spanish and English sit up and take notice, but the whole world.'

'What makes you so sure all of a sudden?' asked Maguire.

'Because Bagenal has assembled a force of two thousand men. Now *we* outnumber them easily. And I'll match or double any wager that not half of that two thousand are real soldiers. But by the time the world hears of it, there will have been double that number and they will all have been the Queen's finest.'

We set out at around nine o'clock in the morning and I felt that we had left it a little late, so we set our pace at a fair lick. Even so, we only managed to reach our destination about half an hour before the enemy and the men were already tired from the forced march. We had little time to prepare for a battle and the English were moving at a decent speed, so we had to attack prematurely.

For three solid hours we fought and finally the enemy broke through and drove onto the Blackwater Fort. It was our own fault. We were positioned very poorly and overconfident of victory. I underestimated Bagenal's determination and resilience. However, all was not lost – they still had to get through us on the way back to Newry. I decided to study the lay of the land in more detail. Red, Maguire, Art, Cormac, Tyrrell and myself ascended a nearby hill where we might get a better perspective of the territory.

'That's where we want them ideally,' said Maguire pointing to the foot of the mountains a few miles away. 'If they can be steered in that direction and driven up into the mountains, we can cut them to pieces at our leisure.'

'Bagenal would suss that plan out immediately,' said Red.

'Yes,' said Maguire jumping in before Red could continue, 'but would he be able to do anything about it?'

'I think he has already proven that he's far more able than we gave him credit for,' replied Red. 'If we tried to implement that plan, he would evade us and break through again like he did this morning. Our forces would have to be spread over that four or five miles there and that is a lot of ground to cover. It would take most of our army to stay down here and drive them up into the mountain. There certainly wouldn't be much of an ambush party left up there.'

Silence reigned for what seemed like an eternity as we all got a good eyeful of the surrounding countryside.

'So what would you suggest, Red?' asked Maguire.

'I'm not sure,' he confessed. 'I have to say that we don't seem to have too many options.'

'The mountain will not work,' said Tyrrell, 'but it's a good idea. We need to get them in an area where they can't manoeuvre very well and where we can surround them.'

'But look around you, Tyrrell,' said Art, 'it's all open country apart from that mountain range.'

'Yes,' replied Tyrrell, 'I know. Maybe we should look elsewhere.'

'We haven't got time,' I said shaking my head. 'And besides, I'm not sure we need to.'

At that everyone started talking at once and pointing this way and that, demonstrating the impossibility of the task.

'Where there's a will...' I said putting up my hand for calm, '...there's a way. Observe, gentlemen, if you will, yonder fields.'

Everyone came closer and looked to where I was pointing about three miles away.

'I think what we have here, gentlemen, is an optical illusion and a perfect opportunity to exploit it.'

'What on earth are you talking about, Hugh?' asked Cormac.

'Well, Red is quite right when he says that Bagenal will suss

Maguire's plan and break through. Tyrrell is also correct in backing Maguire in his view that we need to surround them where they can't move. Well, those fields will be that place.'

The looks on their faces suggested that I had lost my senses.

'Are you serious, Hugh?' asked Maguire.

'Never more so.'

'Ach, come on, Hugh, you're codding us!' said Art.

'I assure you, brother, that I am not. Just look further than those fields to the north and you will see the land dips before the horizon is cut out by the mountains.'

All their faces assumed a look of blank concentration as though they knew exactly what they were looking at but should be seeing something more.

'Gentlemen,' I continued, 'the land dips because it has been cut away. It has been cut away because of the turf. Gentlemen, we have a vast uncut bog. And considering the amount of rainfall we have endured recently, I would suggest that we have potentially a very wet uncut bog. Possibly bordering on swamp conditions.'

Smiles were beginning to creep across some visages.

'Our plan,' I said, 'will be to make them think that we are trying to drive them up into the mountain for an ambush. They will not see the cut bog as they will be coming from the west and their view will be obscured by this beautiful mountain put there by God's own hand. We will defend the line in numbers so it doesn't look too obvious, but we will make our beautiful green bog appear to be the best escape route. And once they have broken through our line and fallen into the trap, we will launch our main offensive from three sides. The rear where they have just broken through. Their right flank which is that scrubby wood yonder. Unfortunately, it's a bit too sparse so we won't be able to dedicate too many resources over there – we'll just fight a holding action there. And finally, the left flank which is the visually hidden cut bog, which will provide a vast wall for cover. Any questions?'

They all shook their heads smiling.

'All agreed?'

'Yes,' they all replied in unison.

'Well, before we decide completely, let's check that it is indeed our bog of dreams.'

Chapter X
CLONTIBRET

All was quiet that night but I could sense an uneasy tension in our sentries. It seems they felt that the enemy might try to sneak past us under the cover of darkness. This was good news for us as it made sleep impossible for them and served to further heighten their senses. However, dawn rubbed the sleep from her eyes unmolested and we were free to prepare properly.

After a light breakfast we took up our positions and waited. That was all we could do. It's amazing how time seems to stand still when you are waiting for something to happen. It seemed to take the sun years to work its way across the sky that morning. I think the most difficult aspect of that morning was the silence. It was imperative that we kept quiet and not give the game away to the enemy. That was incredibly difficult – sitting around for hours without saying anything. The silence took on an eerie presence almost as if it was reading my thoughts. In fact, not just my thoughts. I'm sure everybody was thinking the same things. It is only in the absence of conversation and interaction that you realise how little you take time out to think on a daily basis. Well, on that 27 May 1595, we all had plenty of time for thought. And it was far from pleasant. I believe humans to be pessimistic by nature and when you are forced to confront your inner demons you tend to focus on worst-case scenarios. I must have died hundreds of times in my mind that morning in the cruellest of fashions. The English managed to fight off our attack and turn it into a counter-offensive and destroy us. I saw Red hunted like a dog and hacked to pieces. I was held down by eight to ten Englishmen completely helpless as they slowly cut parts of me away before hacking off my tongue and my nose, and then gouging out my eyes and leaving me to bleed to death.

I tried to turn my thoughts to victory, and each time I

managed to see my army triumphant, was as they watched me slay Bagenal with my own bare hands. That was a great feeling. However, it wasn't long before the nightmares grim returned to chase away the dreams sweet and I was being tortured to death once more.

My thoughts were eventually interrupted by a patrol, which galloped into Clontibret. The officer in charge dismounted and ran over to me.

'My Lord,' he said saluting me formally.

'What news?' I asked.

'The enemy began breaking camp about twenty minutes ago, my Lord. We watched for about ten minutes to ensure that this was the case and then returned with all haste.'

'How far is this camp?'

'About three miles due west, my Lord.'

'Well, that's consistent with the reports from last night's patrols. How long do you estimate it will take them to get here?'

'I expect we will see the first of them in about an hour, my Lord.'

'Good. Anything else?'

'No, my Lord.'

'Very good. You have done well,' I said. 'Take your men and horses up yonder mountain for some food and rest. Seamus here will guide you to the camp.'

'But, my Lord, the battle?' said the officer almost crestfallen.

'You have played a big enough role already, man. You have provided us with the invaluable information, which will enable us to secure victory this day. You and your men have had no sleep and are clearly tired. Your rest is well earned and thoroughly deserved. And besides, there will be other battles. You will get your chance to spill blood. But now you must rest.'

By this time he was staring at the ground in disappointment but he nodded in agreement.

'Yes, my Lord,' he said. 'Thank you, my Lord.'

And with that he bowed and left to lead his men into the hill. As he and his men went, many of the men waiting for battle patted them on the backs or shook them by the hands in thanks for what they had done. Surely appreciation above more than mere words can say. I turned to my signalman with a renewed pride and confidence, all thoughts of defeat and death despatched from my mind.

'Send the signal of one hour to the others,' I ordered.

The signalman did as he was bade, and in the hill, by the cut bog and by the scrub, a solitary signalman in each position acknowledged receipt of the message. Once I knew that Red, Maguire, Tyrrell and MacMahon had received the news, I turned to my ever-silent troops just as they turned to theirs.

'Men,' I began, 'today the Lord smiles upon us. He gives us strength for battle. He gives us absolution in our hearts. And he gives us answers to our prayers. We have chosen the perfect ground. We have chosen the perfect battle plan. And we have chosen the path of Our Lord. We all know what we must do. Discipline will win the day. Let's show the same sort of commitment and control we displayed at the Ford of the Biscuits and let's send the English to Hell again. The enemy will be with us in an hour. Silence and patience will be our first weapons. Follow your orders and victory will be ours. I hope to raise a drink in celebration with all of you after the battle. But now let us join Father Mullins in prayer.'

The priest came and stood on my right-hand side.

'Lord, hear the prayers of your faithful soldiers of Ireland and help them prevail in the battle ahead,' he prayed.

Every man then blessed himself and uttered a silent 'Amen,' then retook their positions and waited once more. There was certainly a sense of fear in the air. Nobody wants to die. But it's a strange thing, even though nobody wants to die and everyone has a healthy fear of death, in battle no man is afraid of confronting the prospect. It's difficult to explain and I think one must experience it to appreciate it fully. Our own mortality is our greatest fear, yet when we are in greatest danger of losing our lives, we don't avoid it but race to meet it head on. Why? I don't suppose I'll ever know. But even though it was deathly silent in that hour before the battle, it had the same atmosphere as any battle I had fought in previously, even though every battle before that was preceded by a great cacophony of taunting and jeering. It's difficult to describe but it's a mixture of fear and determination, of guilt and pride, of hate and desire. It's like no other emotion and I defy anyone to claim otherwise. I also defy anyone to claim that their stomach remains calm before a battle. I remember the first time I took to the field in conflict, I could not eat in the hours before the fight. And that proved to be a mistake because as soon as the enemy came into view I vomited for a full five minutes. And because my stomach was empty, I could only summon up bile, which I then tasted for the seven hours' duration of the battle. Ever since then I have forced myself to eat a hearty meal before any battle, so that when the time comes, my stomach has something substantial to offer. Battle certainly does something to people that nothing else can.

It is also very odd how time becomes distorted. I remember that day at Clontibret thinking that the hour we were waiting for the enemy was the longest I have ever experienced. And yet when I look back, it seems that before we knew it we could hear them in the distance: that unmistakeable sound of an army on the move. When we first heard the faint rumbling from afar, the silence amongst us grew ever more eerie. However, when we caught our first glimpse of their colours that was when the puking started. I'm telling you it just cannot be helped. You get this sudden grim realisation, even though you have been thinking of nothing else for hours, that here and now you may breathe your last. Grown men have been known to soil themselves, not just in their first battle, but every time.

When the English were close enough to view the full column but still far away enough that they had not yet spotted us in our sparse cover, I sent one hundred light cavalry in to charge around from their right flank in front of their van and swirl off, drawing some infantry off in pursuit, which were subsequently left open for target by our infantry. As the English gathered together a charge, I sent another feinting attack from the cavalry with light infantry running at the stirrup, which once again skirted and stabbed at their right flank. At the same time I gave the order for our ranks in the front and along our left (the enemy's right flank) to fire off a volley. We were just out of range, but that was deliberate. The enemy's left flank was skirting the foot of the mountain now and some were even breaking off and moving up into the cover. I wanted to give Bagenal the impression that we were trying to drive them into the hills. He took the bait. He withdrew his cavalry from their attempted engagement of our own and regrouped his men as best he could with the aim of driving into our heart and through the open fields. His orders were quite clear for all to see that under no circumstances were his forces to seek cover in the hills. He then gave the order to drive forward. This began slowly and my men were superb in conducting our charade of beating a slow and reluctant retreat until our line broke and we scattered either side. Once Bagenal achieved the breakthrough, his charge gained pace and momentum but he could not stop some of his ranks from giving chase to our troops as they scattered. His men obviously had the smell of victory in their nostrils and were keen to slay some rebels for Her Majesty, whereas Bagenal, all credit to him, merely wanted to drive on and put distance between themselves and us. His poor, misfortunate soldiers who gave chase to the apparently fleeing Irish ran straight into our cavalry who hacked them to pieces in minutes.

The English advance was gathering pace, and even though Bagenal had lost some poor fools who had charged off in the quest for glory, he must have been feeling quite pleased with himself that he had not fallen for the obvious trap and had managed to push through and reach relative safety. As his rearguard passed the point where our ranks had broken, our forces who had sent the volley of fire from our left, swung around behind the enemy and joined together with the small force in the mountain to close the retreat door on the English. Within a couple of minutes after that the English discovered, much to their horror, what our real trap was. Their wagons were sinking in the bog and their horses could not negotiate the terrain beyond a plodding trot. Even the infantry were hampered by the soft ground. We, in contrast, merely skirted the bog itself and formed tight walls of gunfire on three sides of the enemy – both flanks and the rearguard. On the enemy's left flank, now they had moved past the foot of the mountain, Red's men were able to fire wilfully on the English from the cut bog. Maguire and MacMahon menaced the enemy from the scrub on their right flank, while I and my brothers made retreat impossible at their rear. We also managed to muster a small combined force to take up position at the enemy's van, but as the area was quite open we could not afford to send any real strength to the front. The same tactics were employed throughout the battle with constant fire coming undercover from all sides of the English. We also kept sending in horse and foot striking and swirling and drawing off some enemy in pursuit, who would then be trapped and destroyed by another force. This must have infuriated Bagenal, but there really was nothing he could do about it. His men were trapped like rats. They were frightened, tired and panicked. It was small wonder that some of them were losing their minds.

All of a sudden one of Bagenal's officers in the rearguard seized the initiative and gathered a force of his men together. He drove back towards my position where the enemy had come from in order to try and punch a hole in our line and weaken our position in their rear. Fierce fighting ensued and many engaged in hand-to-hand single combat. We defended our line like lions and they tried to drive through like a herd of buffalo. Many brave men on both sides fell in this engagement.

And then it happened. It's extremely odd. When most men recount the tale of the time they killed another in hand-to-hand combat, they can take the listener through each and every move, thrust and parry from the birth of the engagement to its death. They tend to remember details like the colour of the opponent's eyes and hair, his height, his build, his armour, distinguishing features such as scars and moles and other trivia like his stance and which hand he favoured. They can take the listener through the story blow-by-blow and describe any injuries sustained during the course of the encounter in graphic detail. They invariably always seem to be marathon duels, which take centre stage of the battle as the two opponents are left to their own devices by the respective armies.

I killed a man in hand-to-hand combat at Clontibret and I don't remember anything. I could not tell you anything about my victim. I can't remember if there was a struggle. It is entirely beyond my powers of memory to recall how long it lasted. Was I in danger at any point? Who knows? The only thing I can tell you is that I wasn't there. Physically, I did it all, but my mind was elsewhere. For however long it took, my body acted without the command of my brain.

Everything had gone according to plan. The English had fallen into our trap and we were in complete control. But their drive threatened our victory. And then something snapped inside me. Suddenly all the years of frustration and anger boiled up inside me and I saw my chance to gain some revenge. And so, as the battle crawled slowly closer and closer as the English tried to punch their way through our line, I got directly involved in the fighting. The next thing I knew my victim slumped against me propped up by my sword through his belly and out his back. I withdrew my weapon and he collapsed moaning. I felt sick. I truly don't know how much time had passed or what had happened. All I knew was I had lost control and it frightened me. So, I scanned the scene quickly, decided on our course of action, issued the appropriate orders and retreated to a position where I could monitor the progress of the battle.

And soon we were reorganised and gaining the upper hand once more. We were slowly pushing the enemy back and it became all too apparent that their initiative had failed and so the officer in charge ordered the retreat and they made to rejoin their column.

The English did manage to keep moving, all credit to them. But the terrain made it painfully slow for them and we were able to pick them off knowing time and conditions were on our side. It also soon became obvious that they were running low on ammunition as they refused to fire at our positions of cover and waited instead for our sporadic lightning attacks. All in all the main battle lasted for at least seven or eight hours and we pursued them all the way to Newry after that.

Clontibret proved to be a magnificent victory for us. The official English casualties were only a few hundred but they had a habit of not counting churls and kerne. They also understated their losses so they could still claim wages and provisions. After we drew off our troops from the battle, we retreated to Fortress Ulster safe in the knowledge that the enemy would be too busy licking their wounds to bother us for a while.

It was time to raise that drink we hoped we would share after the battle. And it was time to wait for news of how Clontibret was received.

Chapter XI
THE REAL O'NEILL

The reaction to the Ford of the Biscuits, as I have said before, was incredible. However, it paled into insignificance alongside the phenomenal reaction to events at Clontibret. All of a sudden it seemed that everyone was taking an interest. In all honesty I do not think that anyone directly involved in the war was too surprised with our victory – even the English. We all knew that the enemy was ill-equipped, poorly trained, disease-ridden and lacked motivation, and that we had all the advantages. But the world outside of Ireland could not bring itself to believe that an English Army could be defeated by a 'rebellious rabble' quite so easily and convincingly. Our rabble was beginning to take on a persona all of its own doused in wonder, awe and vicious rumours.

Indeed the mysticism surrounding myself that I was trying so desperately to cultivate seemed to have a life of its own at this stage. It was obviously further heightened by two major victories on the battlefield and Elizabeth's embarrassing agreement of Dublin. These events were viewed more or less as miracles, and rumours of my powers spread like wildfire. Obviously, I had generated many rumours of my own early on but now they seemed to spring up out of the very land! I think my favourite fabrication was that I was a master of disguise and held a position at the Queen's Court, which explained how I always knew what the Sassenachs were going to do. But more than that, I was actually the Virgin Queen's lover! I have absolutely no idea where the rumours originated but I was eternally thankful. Nobody knew what to believe about me anymore. Was O'Neill really in league with Beelzebub or was he really a puppet for O'Donnell? The truth no longer mattered. My name struck fear into the heart of every English soldier and made everyone else extremely wary of me. Who knows, if the stories were true, maybe I would eat their babies in the dead of night, after all!

Elizabeth was absolutely furious with their lack of progress against us and flabbergasted that they had suffered another defeat at Clontibret. Her worst nightmares could not have prepared her for such an event after the Biscuits. She just could not understand how some of her best military leaders – who had brought her so much glory on the continent – could founder against a bunch of ill-disciplined savages. And as long as her attitude remained as such, then all the Court and kingdom and much of the world would share that opinion. And that was fine by me. For if she remained so blind to the situation, then I would continue to enjoy the upper hand. Let her sniff the air in contempt and adopt her aloof and superior attitude. If she thought of us as muck savages for long enough, we would surely shift her bony arse from the throne!

However, no matter what her councillors said in front of her, I knew they were secretly worried. The army in Ireland was dead on its feet. It could not get anywhere near its enemy and its commanders were being outwitted at every turn. They also knew we were courting Spain. Their worst fears, they felt, could soon be realised: that Ireland may be lost from England and would be used as a base for Spain. In short, the council knew they were in more danger now than ever before. Clontibret had truly brought the terror to them.

I was delighted with how Clontibret was received by all and I had yet to hear from Spain. Alonso was due to land any day and I counted down the minutes awaiting his arrival.

Chapter XII
ARROGANCE

The arrogant bastards! After everything that has happened so far in this conflict – the Ford of the Biscuits, the Dublin agreement, Clontibret – everything that has all gone our way and been an unmitigated disaster for the English, they still maintain their aloof and superior stance. I am convinced that they truly believe they have a divine right to win. I have written to them courting peace twice, and on both occasions they have returned my correspondence unopened!

Well, that attitude will only serve to contribute to their downfall. If they continue to refuse to acknowledge the threat that we pose to their administration, it will go the worse for them. Their destruction will be complete long before they act in an appropriate manner. I intend to choke them with their own arrogance.

Chapter XIII
REWRITING HISTORY

What do these English expect? They malign my good name because I refuse to face them in open field. I choose to use my natural resources to good effect. We have dense forest, rugged coastline, wild, deep rivers and more mountains than you can shake a stick at. These combine to provide a beautiful, yet awesome, natural barrier, which hold the enemy at bay. I use them as assets in our struggle. Who would not?

But the English view this as cheating. They call me coward, traitor, hill-hopper and other degrading titles, and all because they want a fair fight. A fair fight, of course, means that they have greater numbers, superior weapons, a navy as opposed to our distinct lack of one, the option to buy a couple of traitors in our camp and the right to call a foul move if we manage to deliver a blow against them. I don't know what would make them happy! Maybe we should just fling spuds at them!

Also they get to choose a nice open field where we can all see each other. Apart from the generals, of course, who will view the whole spectacle through an eyeglass a couple of miles away while drinking tea shipped from India. Having said that, because of the miser chilling the throne with her bony arse, we actually outnumber them at the moment, so that, of course, would be unfair.

It makes me despair sometimes. Can they not see that the unfairness and injustice is their being here in the first place? No, of course, they can't! They believe they have a divine right to rule. Bastards, the lot of them!

Their latest move in muddying my name was inevitable – the proclamation. So now I am officially a traitor! Marvellous! Now I can give full vent to my spleen. It is almost perverse. The English love to use tradition and precedent as weapons and yet shy away from them when it suits their own devious needs. They have conducted the whole charade of delivering this proclamation according to the rules, just so they have an excuse for their actions to come. Which is to say that they can claim to be blameless when they start the butchering. But they gloss over the fact that they have conveniently changed history to suit their story.

Lord Burghley himself drafted the proclamation, and it has been announced in every town from Dublin to Dundalk so far. But now its progress has been delayed so that it can coincide with their army's march into Ulster. Over my dead and decaying corpse! But then, that's their general idea, I believe!

'Tis a hypocritical little piece of filth. For as long as anyone can remember, my father was seen by the Crown as a loyal, brave and respected upholder of the English ways in the face of much adversity. However, according to this document, he has been labelled a coward, a bastard and a snidey, untrustworthy Gaelic rebel! What imaginations these people possess! Even more incredible is their assessment of Tirleach Luineach. The man has been miraculously transformed from a snivelling scumbag into a noble gentleman of high morals! Truly remarkable! And Burghley also has the gall and audacity to suggest that I owe everything to Elizabeth! If any fool believes that then they deserve to die by my sword.

However, the amusement of the piece does not stop there. They have accused me of courting Spain and involving other Gaelic lords in rebellion – which is true – but so that I can fulfil my aims of becoming 'Prince of Ulster'. Have they no vision? Can they not see that driving them out and taking all of Ireland is my only option? I cannot believe that they find me so much lacking in ambition. I despair at their lack of foresight, I really do. Is this really the most powerful nation in the world?

The rest of the proclamation was the usual malarkey about pardons for those who desert me. However, I was highly insulted by the lack of a price on my head. I would have thought that the head of the 'Hopping Divil' would be worth at least a few shillings!

I wasn't too bothered about their lame proclamation. Even after its arrival in Ulster when it had been amended to include the events at Clontibret.

I knew I was really beginning to annoy them.

Chapter XIV
LIBERTY OF CONSCIENCE

However, they had been annoyed into action. As I said, they delayed the proclamation's announcement in Ulster until they were ready to mount an assault of sorts. This happened a little sooner than expected. Sir John Norris had been put in charge of the 'Ulster situation' in addition to his duties as commander of the Crown's forces in Ireland. In fairness to him, he moved quicker than I anticipated and I was not quite prepared for him to move on the province in the manner in which he did. His great gusto, energy and enthusiasm urged his men along against all adversity and they were soon ready to strike at us.

For the first time in quite a while it gave me cause for concern and so I took pre-emptive action. I destroyed my home of Dungannon Castle and did the same with the homes of the O'Quinns and the O'Hagans. We could ill-afford for the English to gain a stronghold in our territory. In the meantime we could gain solace and shelter in the homes of our kinsmen. Unfortunately, I made a serious error in not destroying Armagh Cathedral, which the enemy secured easily and committed the ultimate sacrilege of using this holy ground as a base for war.

Even though this oversight on my part was a mistake, I was content to sit in Fortress Ulster, monitor the situation and await developments. It transpired that a lack of draught horses meant that Norris had to return to the Pale for more supplies while the Armagh garrison awaited his return. Obviously, this slowed their progress significantly and enabled me to indulge in a wee touch of mischief. We attacked about midway between Newry and Armagh with a force of horse. 'Twas but a wee skirmish but it delivered the right warning message. In addition, before our men were driven off, Norris himself was wounded in the arm and his brother received a bullet to the leg. Also, some days afterwards I learned that Sir Geoffrey Fenton had drawn up a report of the engagement which suggested that our cavalry were far more enterprising than their English counterparts – praise indeed!

It soon became apparent that the initial enthusiasm that accompanied the English move had evaporated into thin air and they were as demoralised and disillusioned as ever. The infighting and bickering among their senior officers was beginning to take its toll and was filtering through the ranks. Norris and Russell, the Lord Deputy at the time, hated the sight of one another and, after one spectacular argument, Russell withdrew to the Pale in a sulk and left Norris in full control of the army.

Even though they considered us to be a serious threat, in my opinion they needed to look in a mirror to find their most dangerous enemy.

Having said that, it was now September and the harvest needed to be gathered – preferably without hindrance. We had still not received anything other than comforting and supportive words from King Philip II and I dearly wished to avoid a winter campaign. The enemy was in no fit state to mount a serious threat in the winter but I wanted to ensure that they would not even attempt anything. With this in mind I sent a short submission to Norris on behalf of my family, my allies, my followers and, of course, myself. This, as I suspected it would be, was rejected outright, as he disliked my claim of jurisdiction over all the northern lords. It mattered not. That was my aim in this correspondence – to let him know that I was in control. Once it was dismissed, I submitted an amended version, which spoke only for myself and my family. I acknowledged my offences, renounced my Gaelic title of O'Neill in favour of my anglicised title of the Earl of Tyrone, and I requested a pardon. Red and all the other lords did likewise and these were duly accepted. Ten days later a truce was agreed, in spite of our difference over the revictualling of Armagh.

This truce was nothing more than a political game for both sides. Neither we nor the English saw it as a step in the right direction towards peace but a method of buying time and preparing for the next phase of the war. We humans are a bizarre species made stranger still by our insistence on following diplomacy and politics through to an unnatural end.

As far as I was concerned, I would demand just enough to make long term agreement impossible. I could not very well inform my enemy that my ultimate aim was to drive them into the sea with or without Spanish assistance. I could not allow them to know the full extent of my plans. What I would do then was assure them that I was hungry for peace and the opportunity to live once more under the protection of Her Majesty's wing, but under vastly altered conditions and circumstances. And I needed to ensure that the demands I outlined would be unacceptable to the point that agreement could not be reached but not pushing them far enough to break off negotiations and resume hostilities. I needed time. Sure, we were making great progress and winning the conflict, but the English were a powerful enemy and still had a firm grip on Ireland.

From the English perspective I could see their lies as clearly as the moon in a cloudless night sky. I knew the procedure inside out. Had I not served Elizabeth long enough to know the policies of the Court? They were trying to buy time in much the same fashion as I was but for different reasons. They were trying to buy time because they were ill-prepared to continue the war right now. They were also very wary of Spain. The last thing they wanted was for Ireland to be used as a back door for the Spanish. And so if they could secure a long-term peace, they would. Also, it is much easier to fight an enemy who thinks they are protected by a truce. The English are a famously patient race and they wanted to secure peace and monitor the situation. And then, when we would least expect it and our guard was down, they would strike and reclaim control. They would probably arrest myself, Red, Maguire and all the other powerful lords on trumped up charges of treason. And then they would reclaim all they had lost and more besides with virtually no fighting, if it could be avoided. Had they not done exactly that very thing to Shane, my uncle? Had they not done this to Desmond? Had they not done it to Red's father? In fact, they had done this so many times, it was simply a matter of course to them.

The truce was set to remain in place until the dawn of the new year and we were to meet in order to try to reach agreement before then. However, even though there was no real attempt at this time by either side to gain ground in the struggle, minor skirmishes were inevitable and ensued frequently. This only served to add more ridicule to the whole charade as both we and the English complained that the other side was breaking the truce.

For one reason or another – mainly because I delayed as much as I could – we never actually met the enemy until January 1596. This meeting was also a cause of embarrassment and humiliation for Elizabeth, as I refused resolutely to meet in Dundalk itself, and so our chat was conducted in a field a couple of miles outside the town. Sir Henry Wallop and Sir Robert Gardiner led the English contingent, and myself and Red spoke for our cause. 'Twas a bizarre scene with the parley taking place in the middle of the field between men armed only with swords. We had two English officers camped between the parley and our army, and we had two of our own officers offering a mirror service to the English.

'My Lords,' I said bowing, and Red repeated the greeting after me.

'My Lords,' replied Wallop and Gardiner in unison. 'Have you read the terms?' demanded Wallop.

'We have, my Lord,' I responded.

'And do you agree?' asked Gardiner.

'No!' said Red simply.

'No, sir?' demanded Wallop.

'No,' repeated Red evenly staring at Wallop with steel.

'Do you wish to come to a bloody end, Lord O'Donnell?' spat Wallop.

'My Lord Wallop,' I interjected, 'my colleague Lord O'Donnell merely means that there are elements of the agreement we wish to discuss. Now surely we are at liberty to do so, otherwise there is no point to this meeting.'

'Of course, my Lord O'Neill,' said Gardiner before Wallop could vent his spleen again. 'Now which elements do you feel are unjust?'

'Well, my Lord Gardiner,' I replied, 'I am afraid that the garrison of Armagh is extremely distasteful to me and poses a real threat to my peace of mind. Also, I am afraid that I cannot set free the MacShanes in my custody for fear of the harm that will befall my country from those Scots should I do so.'

'Well, my Lord O'Neill,' replied Gardiner, 'I'm sure we can come to a mutual agreement—'

'What?' bellowed Wallop. 'Would you so easily succumb to traitors, my Lord Gardiner? I will not allow my queen to be dictated to by a simple savage with the morals of a rat…'

'Why not?' said Red. 'I can see that she employs rats to do her negotiating on her behalf!'

'How dare you, sir!' barked Wallop drawing his sword. 'I'll run you through for that, you dog!'

'Lord Wallop!' screamed Gardiner putting his hand on Wallop's arm and restraining him and all the while Red sat on his horse stone-faced. 'May I have a moment in private, my Lords, with my colleague?' asked Gardiner of us as he held Wallop back.

'Of course, my Lord Gardiner,' I replied graciously. 'Take all the time you need.'

Gardiner led Wallop away beyond earshot, which gave Red and myself an opportunity to have a quiet word ourselves.

'What are those bastards cooking up?' asked Red, eyeing them savagely.

'Never mind about them,' I replied. 'Gardiner is just trying to restore Wallop to calm because they feel that it is essential that they reach agreement here today. They are shitting themselves, Red. They don't have the money to deal with the war right now because of their commitments abroad. They know that Spain poses a potentially lethal threat through us and so Elizabeth wants to appease us more than anything else right now. We have a golden opportunity to see how far we can push the bastards.'

'Fine,' replied Red. 'I'm all in favour of pushing them.'

'Steady, Red,' I warned. 'We are not in the greatest position ourselves,' I said. The last thing I wanted to do was allow Red to become overconfident, so I felt I needed to stress the dangers. 'We need Spain but they are not in our corner yet. We must be cautious. Let's just remain calm today and push them as far as we can without the negotiations falling through.'

'All right, Hugh,' he conceded and we broke from our talk to return to Wallop and Gardiner who had also finished their chat.

Wallop was seething but he never said another word that day and just left the talking to Gardiner.

'My Lords,' said Gardiner, 'having consulted Lord Wallop, we have decided to propose to Her Majesty that the MacShanes remain in your custody, which I am certain she will agree to. However, on the question of the Armagh garrison, we can only relay your concerns, my Lord Tyrone, and await instruction from Her Majesty.'

'I am sure that my Lords will do their best,' I said. 'However, we do have other concerns regarding your terms, my Lord Gardiner.'

'Oh, yes?' he asked.

'I am afraid that I cannot accept a President of Ulster who will, no doubt, sheriff the province unfairly, my Lord Gardiner. Also, there is no way in this world or the next that I can offer my son as a hostage. However, I am prepared to offer a son of O'Hagan to be held until peace is completed,' I said, knowing that I would never send in one of my dear friend's sons.

'These are strong terms you are rejecting, my Lord Tyrone,' replied Gardiner. 'We see them as essential to ensure your behaviour, my Lord.'

'And who ensures your behaviour, my Lord Gardiner?' demanded Red.

'It is *you* who are rebelling, my Lord Tir Connell, not us,' came the tart reply.

'So we must behave even though you have invaded our country and even now enforce your ways and religious beliefs on us. Tell me, Lord Gardiner, which is the greater wrong in your eyes: the theft and rape of a culture or the defence of it?'

'You are twisting the truth, my Lord Tir Connell,' said Gardiner. 'We English have not done anything that has not been invited by the Irish. It is only natural that the Gaelic ways will eventually be replaced by the more modern English ways.'

'Really?' demanded Red.

'Yes,' said Gardiner.

'Well, I never asked you on to my lands, Gardiner,' retorted Red. 'I love the Gaelic ways and wish to worship the Lord Jesus Christ in the Catholic Church. I care not for the English, and if that is not plain enough for you, if you still think you are invited to the party, then allow me to make myself understood: turn around and fuck off back to England!'

'My Lord Tir Connell!' said Gardiner. 'If it were not for Lord Tyrone's desire for peace, I would turn from this parley now and make ready for war!'

'If you want war, then let's make war,' said Red. 'If you want peace, then let's parley. But don't use my Lord O'Neill as an excuse for your actions. And don't expect us to lay down and just accept your derogatory terms. The whole reason for the conflict is because we are unhappy with the situation in the north, so going back to that state of affairs is totally unacceptable from the outset. Are you too blind to see that, Gardiner?'

Red was really winding them up and Wallop could barely contain himself. He looked like he was going to explode. Gardiner was also getting more insulted and upset as the proceedings wore on.

'All right, my Lords,' said Gardiner, 'I will endeavour to abolish the appointment of a President of Ulster, but if we are not to have the son of my Lord Tyrone, then one son of O'Hagan will not suffice.'

'I'll deliver four sons of O'Hagan,' I said, knowing that if I was never going to send one of his sons, then I would certainly never send four.

'Agreed,' said Gardiner.

'Not so fast,' I said. 'I will deliver four of O'Hagan's sons as long as my Lord Gardiner guarantees that there will be no President of Ulster. Merely endeavouring is not good enough – there must be a guarantee that this will not happen.'

'Agreed,' said Gardiner once again as he visibly sagged. 'If that is all, my Lords, then you will excuse us as we have much to prepare for Her Majesty.' He began to turn his horse to go when Red stopped him in his tracks.

'Does my Lord Gardiner seriously believe that we would not wish to alter the religious situation?' demanded Red.

'In what way, my Lord Tir Connell?' asked Gardiner.

'We want liberty of conscience added to the amendments, my Lord Gardiner,' replied Red. The practice of Catholicism had been banned in Ireland a long time before this and liberty of conscience was but a flowery term for the freedom to practice our chosen religion.

'It will be done,' said Gardiner wearily.

'For *all* Irishmen,' added Red.

'My Lord Tir Connell!' blasted Gardiner. 'Please desist from these excessive demands. Her Majesty will not stand for it. I will arrange for liberty of conscience for my Lords Tyrone and Tir Connell but no others.' And with that he turned his horse and galloped away before Red could issue any other demands.

The next day we met again and reached agreement. Pardons were to be issued for myself and Red but we put off receiving them until the spring. It was clear for all to see that both sides just wanted a break from the fighting for different reasons and that the truce would not last.

In the meantime, even though negotiations were in full flow, hostilities did not cease. While both sides trod carefully and probed warily, there were inevitably some clashes. In one such instance, Lord Chichester came upon a body of a few hundred Scottish mercenaries and almost jokingly suggested an attack to his officers. They, however, were only too willing to accept and so they launched a charge. In the early exchanges Chichester was shot through the head and the English, without a sole leader, soon became disorganised and confused. The Scots routed their enemy and scored a surprise victory. And the bizarre thing was that the Scots were making ready to parley and did not want to fight.

In another instance, a garrison from Philipstown came upon Richard Tyrrell's force and launched an attack. Tyrrell soon had them on the run and but twenty escaped death. Again Tyrrell was not looking for a fight.

Yet the English wanted peace?

Chapter XV
CADIZ

I received some news today that put our position into stark perspective. And even though this news is bordering on disastrous, it may serve to keep some feet on the ground. Of course, the men should be proud of what we have achieved so far on our own. But we must retain our composure and caution as even with the aid of Spain, this war is far from a foregone conclusion.

The English are still very much masters of the wave and that is official. Sir Howard of Effingham has led an English fleet to Cadiz where they launched a surprise attack, which also confirms their status as the masters of the underhanded tactics. And they have the gall to suggest that we don't fight fairly. Sometimes I just despair at the lunacy of this world and I cannot make sense of it. But I digress. This attack proved to be more successful than even the English could ever have dreamed. Apparently, the Spanish barely put up a fight and many ships were torched and sunk. Effingham sacked the town for seventeen days, destroying everything for miles around until the Spaniards eventually rallied and returned to reclaim their town. Stories suggest that the invaders behaved like perfect gentlemen and respected holy ground and the virtue of the women. Which means that they behaved like perfect gentlemen apart from the surprise attack, the murdering, the pillaging, the plundering and all that goes with an invasion.

This was a bitter blow for us as well as the Spanish. As I have already suggested, England now had no rival to the sea worthy of the name.

The Spanish fleet was severely damaged by this attack and the English were, no doubt, delighted with the success of the expedition. Obviously, the Spanish fleet would be considered a worthy target for the English anyway, but rumour has it that it was decided to attack Cadiz to eradicate the threat of a Spanish landing in Ireland. Ironically, I believe that on this occasion the fleet was not destined for our shores.

However, it says an awful lot about the English military mind. They did not relish the fight in Ireland. They knew that it entailed hunger, disease, desertion and a host of other unsavoury conditions. And the English never got to choose the battleground in our campaign – and the English dearly like to dictate play. Therefore, they would much rather face a militarily stronger foe than us if they only got to choose the ground. So on the face of it, to attack the fleet in Cadiz in order to help their cause in Ireland may seem bizarre in the extreme, but the plan, as has been proved, has merit.

I suppose in a way we should see this as a great compliment to the threat we pose and the tactics we employ. But I am too realistic to see it other than what it is – a massive setback.

Chapter XVI
INAUGURATION

It was the proudest day of my life. I sat upon the stone throne of Tullahogue where my inauguration as the O'Neill would take place, and my mind drifted. Though awake, I dreamt. My mind raced back to the days when my forefathers ruled all of Ireland as Ard Rí, High Kings from Tara. The O'Neill clan was always the most powerful in the country and we were generally fair rulers. The Irish were a happy people then, content with life and at peace with one another. We were the leading light of the world – the land of saints and scholars. The rest of Europe suffered with a black cloud hanging over the land during these dark ages. But Ireland shone her torch and led the way for Europe to follow into the age of enlightenment. And then the Vikings came and brave Brian Boru drove them into the sea at Clontarf. And then the Normans came, but alas, there was no Brian Boru to repel them. And we O'Neills lost our power and were reduced to Tyrone and some lands beyond.

Then I thought of my father Matthew and how we, the O'Neills, always seemed to quarrel with the O'Donnells. And how my uncle Shane murdered my father and so, unbelievable as it may seem, we were quarrelling amongst ourselves! How ridiculous we must have seemed from the outside, ripping each other apart when we had common enemies to deal with in the O'Donnells. But where is my head? The O'Donnells? We once ruled all of Ireland and we now worry about a tiny portion of the country. Surely we share a common enemy with the O'Donnells – the English.

And then I woke from my dream just as the investiture ended. I had prepared a speech, which was now useless. I had had a vision and I was determined that my vision would be my fate.

It was time to show my true colours. I would use my

appointment as the O'Neill in a symbolic gesture, which would reject my English connections forever. From this day forth I would wear only Gaelic clothes, follow only Gaelic customs and speak only the Gaelic tongue (apart from parleys with the enemy where it would be churlish and childish not to speak English).

Chapter XVII
MY ORACLE – 1596

The delicate nature of proceedings at this time gave me much room and food for thought. I am convinced that every single one of us has a limit regarding mental pressure. I would imagine that it also depends on the individual in question but that each person has a tolerance level that cannot be exceeded. And once the metaphorical foot does cross that threshold, then insanity ensues. Much like in a physical sense where the body can take only so much before it breaks and each being can withstand different levels, so the mind can take only so much pressure. I only wish I could prove my theory, but alas, I have no evidence whatsoever to substantiate my claims. I only know that during the entire conflict there were times when I felt myself on the verge of madness. Who knows, perhaps at times I crossed this verge and explored the realms of insanity.

The bloodshed, the death, the torture, the hunger and famine, the heartache, the loss of dignity and more besides, the hatred, the vengeance, the savagery and all of the suffering in all of its forms brought about by this tragedy of a war bore heavy in my heart. For I knew that I was guilty of many atrocities and I was also one of the main protagonists who brought this tragedy to life. With certainty I can say that it was not entirely my fault but I had played a big enough role in its birth and execution thereafter. And I was directing proceedings more than any other. The knowledge that no matter what decision you make, people will suffer and die, is a huge responsibility and one that I did not cherish. And there was no end to the tragedy in sight. Our struggle was dragging. Everybody was tired of the whole thing but resolved to continue for the cause.

I truly felt that at times I was losing my mind. Was I really causing all these events to happen? Did I truly have this power to wield at my will? Was I totally in control of this war? Was I justified to pursue my cause? Was I doing it for the right reasons or was it some selfish ego trip? All these questions and more besides haunted my every waking moment. I did not know the answers and it was a struggle to try and separate truth from lies, and fact from fiction.

Indeed, I have no doubt that I would have dived into the depths of despair and madness rather than tiptoe on either side of the border, had it not been for one person – Catherine MacGennis, my fourth wife.

Catherine was my mast upon which I hung my flag. I could not talk to anyone about my dilemmas but Catherine. Red, Maguire, Tyrrell, my brothers, even old man Hovendon was unsuitable for the task, as they were all too caught up in the struggle themselves to take an objective view. Also, I needed to be strong and decisive in their midst lest they develop doubts themselves. But Catherine – Catherine was my oracle. I would consult her and she would advise and encourage me. I have known nobody in my entire life with the wisdom of Catherine. She is truly my guardian goddess sent to this world to protect me from harm.

It is with a great deal of fondness that I recall the memories of our honeymoon on the banks of the Bann. We were staying at Castleroe and taking a break from the ravages of the conflict to such a degree, that I could almost distance myself from the whole tragic affair. Wonderful, wonderful times. But it could not last. I knew this but I did not want to admit it. Eventually, it was Catherine who broached the subject.

'I wonder what my mother is doing at this very moment?' she asked of nobody in particular as she lay on the bank. 'She'll be missing me, no doubt,' she continued. 'Sure, that's only to be expected, she is my mother.'

I remained silent.

'And I miss her,' said Catherine, and I could feel her looking at me even though I lay there with my eyes closed.

'I think I will go and see her tomorrow, Hugh,' she said.

'And cut short our honeymoon?' I asked.

'We have been here a few weeks already, my love,' she replied soothingly. 'And you need to return to our cause.'

Again I remained silent as I gazed at her with what I suppose must have been a doleful look.

'You must!' she said earnestly.

'Let's go away from here,' I said. 'Let's go to the new world of America and make a new start, just you and me.'

'We cannot, Hugh. Your people need you here. You must defeat Elizabeth. We can't desert them now. It's our destiny, our fate. We can't run. Our only chance for true happiness is to stay and fight for what is ours.'

I could feel the tears welling in my eyes. 'Am I doing the right thing?' I asked.

'Of course you are, my love. It is the most noble cause of all to fight for the freedom of a nation. How could it be wrong? The English should not be here – that is undeniable. All the misery and suffering they have brought us through all the years. And you will put a stop to it. I believe in you and I could not be more proud of you.'

I smiled at her lovingly. 'My beautiful Catherine, what would I do without you? You're right. Of course, you're right. You're always right,' I said laughing. 'We must go on. It is the right thing to do. It is the only thing we can do. We will free this nation and we will begin again tomorrow.'

In fact, we began again almost immediately because at that very moment I spied Alonso striding purposefully towards us.

Chapter XVIII
A FLEETING CHANCE

'My Lord O'Neill,' greeted Cobos as he reached us by the river.

'My Lord Cobos,' I responded as I rose from my seat on the bank and walked towards him, arms extended ready for our customary hug and kisses. They are a strange lot these continental Europeans. When greeting old friends they hug each other and kiss on both cheeks. Still, at least it is a friendly custom. And when one thinks about it, what is so strange? I wonder how they would view our custom of wakes for the newly departed? I shudder to think! No doubt we would be labelled mad. So let us be content with the notion that we are all different and that we have our own customs.

Anyway, I digress! Unlike previous occasions, Alonso's hug and kisses were unusually cold. I sensed that all was not well before he said anything.

'My Lord O'Neill,' he began, 'I am afraid I am the bearer of grave news this evening.'

'Oh,' I replied. 'How grave, my Lord Cobos?' I asked.

'Extremely grave, my Lord, and it concerns the fleet that set sail from Cadiz only days ago to assist our struggle.' By this time I felt that Cobos was incredibly passionate about the war and had become embroiled to the degree that he considered it a personal crusade. Indeed, he was spending more time in Ireland than in Spain and was undeniably popular amongst our people.

I liked him very much and he had grown to be a very good friend.

'What news of the fleet?' I asked.

'My Lord, I have received reports that the fleet set sail but was driven back by the weather. The wind changed suddenly and there was nothing they could do. I am sorry, my Lord.'

'It is indeed regrettable, my Lord Cobos,' I replied. 'But there is no need for you to apologise. Fate conspired against us and we must make new plans. That is all. We are still in control of our own destiny and we remain on the brink of victory. With a little luck and a spread of gossip the English will hear that a fleet set sail from Spain. That it did not land in Ireland is of little consequence. The news alone is the threat. And in any case, in real terms we could not take any substantial action until the spring. So worry not, my friend, we will have our day.'

'Perhaps you are correct, my Lord,' replied Cobos. 'But I cannot help feeling that we have somehow missed an opportunity.'

'My friend,' I replied, 'I know that you share our concerns and deeply wish for your own countrymen's involvement, but trust me, it will happen. Worry not about this event. 'Tis but a trifle in the scheme of all things. Now, come! Make ready for a feast. We shall dine tonight and relax safe in our Fortress Ulster.'

'My friend, Lord O'Neill, you are a man of great patience and understanding, and it is an honour to hear your wisdom. I will go and make myself ready for the famous O'Neill and Irish hospitality.'

We hugged and kissed once more and he made for his room back at the castle, which had become a permanent fixture at Castleroe. As he walked away my heart welled with frustration. The cursed weather had betrayed us! I know I had put Alonso's mind at ease but inside this news was a disaster which ate at my very soul. Despite the doubts I may have had, deep down I knew that there was no other way – I just needed Catherine to convince me – and I had planned to take the initiative come the winter with the aid of the Spaniards. The English would not have expected it and I was certain that we could score a victory or two and gain support in the country before the enemy had time to react. And this would have prompted further Spanish assistance.

However, there was little point in dwelling on the subject now. There was nothing we could do. I decided there and then to sit out the winter and resume in the spring. What more could I do?

Chapter XIX

THE STAKES GROW HIGHER – 1597

By the summer of 1597, it was clear that the truce was nothing but a farce. I was quite happy for this state of affairs to continue indefinitely as it brought us more time to court Phillip II. However, it appeared that the English were not willing to allow this situation to continue unaltered. My spies brought news to me in the late spring that they were preparing once more for war. This did not concern me a great deal, but then in the early summer I received a far more worrying report: Russell was being stood down by Burgh. I was not greatly familiar with Burgh but I did know that he was highly regarded by his peers and that he had a mammoth energy and capacity for thought. He would certainly prove to be more enthusiastic about his task than his predecessor.

At the same time they were replacing the cruel Bingham in Connaught with Sir Conyers Clifford. This was certainly a cause for grave concern. I knew Clifford personally. He was an extremely able soldier, an inspiring leader and a fair ruler. He would no doubt bring his charm and honest approach to bear on the local lords and set about winning their support. Bingham had become an asset to us because of his callousness and cruelty to the local people, which meant that it did not take much fuel to spark rebellion. Now the English had reversed their liability by replacing him with Clifford. We would need to keep an eagle's eye on developments in Connaught.

These two changes on the English side did not bode well for us. I decided to call a council so that we could prepare.

It was the first time in quite a few months that we had such a gathering and there was much catching up to be done. Apart from myself and my brothers there was Red, Tyrrell, Maguire, my fosterers during my infancy – the O'Hagans, and the O'Quinns, the O'Cahans, Hovendens, old O'Kane, O'Rourke, MacWilliam

Burke and a number of others including some of my cousins – sons of Shane and Tirleach. We were all united in our common goal, even though some, I felt, still needed some convincing. It was while we were eating, after a glass or two of wine, no doubt, that Maguire decided that his curiosity could wait no more.

'So, O'Neill,' he began, 'I suppose you're going to tell us sooner or later anyway, but why have you decided to call us all together?'

'Aye,' said Red, 'what's going on, Hugh?'

'Gentlemen,' I said rising to my feet, 'as Maguire and Red here have alluded to, there have been developments. So I'm sorry to inform you that I did not bring all of you here so you could eat me out of house and home. Instead, I brought you here to tell you that we have yet another Lord Deputy.'

I had to stop a moment until the cheering subsided. The fact that a new Lord Deputy had been appointed meant that we were making the enemy feel uncomfortable.

'And another one bites the dust, hah!' said Red, laughing.

'What eejit have they sent to get his arse kicked all over the country this time?' asked O'Kane.

'The eejit,' I replied solemnly, 'is Lord Thomas Burgh.'

Silence reigned.

'I judge by your reaction,' I said, 'that you all know of Lord Burgh and his capabilities. You were right, O'Kane, to label his predecessors "eejits", but I think you all realise that this is not the case with Burgh.'

A few of the men nodded their heads, others agreed verbally and more said nothing. But it was clear to see that we all shared the same view that Burgh was dangerous. The stakes were rising.

'At this same time, gentlemen,' I continued, 'there is another new face on the scene. Bingham is being replaced in Connaught by Sir Conyers Clifford.'

I could see by their reactions that some of the men had never heard of Clifford, but others had. And those who had wore a grave countenance indeed.

'So you see, gentlemen,' I said, 'I believe our struggle is about to enter a new stage. The English appear to have tired of the lack of progress in the peace negotiations and seem more than ready to begin a new campaign. As rumour has it, they are doubling their forces over here and are endeavouring to provide proper levels of support and supplies. I have not yet discovered what their plan of action will be but I feel that we are soon to face our biggest challenge yet. I do not believe, no matter how much Cobos suggests it is about to happen, that the Spanish will get reinforcements here in time for the summer. So, once again, it is down to us. We have proven to be more than a match for the English so far and I fail to see why that should change now. But believe me, we must stay vigilant and certainly more alert and prepared than we ever have been before.'

The rest of the feast passed without a word uttered, but as the wine flowed through the evening, so our spirits soared once more. And so again there wasn't a challenge we couldn't accomplish.

The next morning I sent a message each to Red and Maguire in their rooms asking them not to leave until everyone else had gone. I could see they were anxious to find out what I had up my sleeve but they didn't say anything until we were alone.

'What is this all about, O'Neill?' demanded Maguire. 'I have business to attend to and I don't appreciate the delay.'

'Well, Maguire, all will be revealed now,' I replied. 'What do you both know of Clifford?' I asked.

'He has earned a bit of a reputation as a tactician,' replied Maguire honestly.

'Yes, I get the impression that he is something of a thinker,' said Red.

'You're both correct. But he is so much more than that also. I think if it were not for the fact that he is your enemy, that you would like him. He is incredibly charming, extremely funny and likes nothing better than to have a bit of a *craic* with the lads over some wine.'

'So?' said Maguire. 'Are you suggesting that we should go on the piss with the fucker or what?' he asked laughing.

'No, seriously, Maguire, I just want to make sure you both know what you are up against. Red, you have done some tremendous work convincing the lords of Connaught to join us in rebellion. And Hugh, your passion inspires all about you. Clifford possesses the wit and charm to turn them against you once more. Where we used Bingham's cruelty against him, we will be hard-pressed to do anything similar with Clifford. Apart from that, he will prove to be a fair governor and will earn the respect of the people. Christ knows, as an adversary he will earn your respect quick enough! That's the thing about Clifford; you cannot help admiring the man. I know him personally, and I know that of all the English leaders we have had to face up until now, he poses the most lethal threat.'

'Right, well, we will treat him with the respect he deserves,' said Red. 'But we will not fear him, Hugh. We have fought and defeated all sent to crush us so far and I believe we have earned a little respect ourselves. We will be wary of him, but the Lord knows, he had better reciprocate that wariness or it will go hard with him.'

'You have no fears there, Red,' I replied. 'He never underestimates an enemy. Like you said yourself, he is a thinker and he will not move until he has thought it through from every angle.'

'Okay, O'Neill,' said Maguire, 'we consider ourselves warned. But I have a feeling that you have not told us everything that's on your mind.'

'You're right,' I replied with resignation. 'I have been holding something back. But, only because I'm not sure of it myself. It's just a theory I have and I have no proof to substantiate it at all.'

'Go on,' said Maguire. 'You might as well share it with us now.'

'You're right,' I said. 'It can't hurt to let you know my thoughts on these new developments. I think they are getting ready to attack us like they have never attacked before. With Clifford in Connaught and Burgh in the Pale, they have two very able leaders. Also, Burgh is a man of action. I think he will attack us at the Blackwater Fort and, at the same time Clifford will try to cross the Erne from Connaught into Ulster. Now here is the truly worrying part: I don't think Burgh will leave it at that. His two forces would be too far apart, so I think there will be a third force involved in this. But I cannot decide where. He may send this phantom force up through the midlands, so that if they all successfully access Ulster, they can meet up easier than the two forces from the Blackwater and the Erne could otherwise do. However, they may send a naval expedition to land somewhere on the north coast and force us into fighting on two fronts. To be honest, they could try anything, but I think Burgh is too clever to try just the twin attack option. He needs at least three prongs. The only question is where the third prong will come into play.'

'Well, I would say that we just have to prepare for every option,' said Red.

'We can't afford to spread our forces that thin, Red,' said Maguire.

'I don't think we have a choice,' replied Red. 'If we keep our communications network up to scratch, it will only be a matter of a few days for transferring men and we would be ready to meet any number of prongs in their attack. As long as we have large enough forces at the Blackwater and Ballyshannon, we should be fine.'

'That's a risky business, Red,' replied Maguire shaking his head. 'What do you think, O'Neill?'

'Well, I think you are both right,' I began. 'Red, we must endeavour to cover every option, but Maguire's right when he says that it's a risky business. Here's what I suggest though: we leave token forces at strategic points on the coast. Our lack of naval strength means that we would have to meet them on land anyway. You both go and fortify Ballyshannon and cover the Erne as well as possible. I'll stay at the Blackwater. And I'll send Tyrrell with a strong force into Westmeath. My spies should inform me of any developments almost immediately, so we should be able to take action in plenty of time. If the third prong comes through the midlands, I would trust Tyrrell to be able to deal with it or request reinforcements in time to at least slow them enough. My main concern is Clifford. I don't doubt either of you or your abilities, but this fellow is a fox. You must be wary. The only advice I can give is to never panic. If he does try to cross the Erne and manages it... even if he manages to secure a castle or a stronghold, don't panic. His expedition will be totally reliant on the success of the other two because he is so far away from supplies and reinforcements. And I cannot see them achieving victory in one let alone three. But promise me not to let your hearts rule your heads. If you lose your composure, he will destroy you in an instant.'

Both my sons-in-law looked insulted, hurt, but more than anything else they looked concerned. I think they realised I was genuinely worried and I would never mean to insult them. So they made an oath to me and to God that they would cut their losses in the event of a reverse. And I took them at their word. But I was still worried. They were proud men who succumbed all too easily to the red mist. Yes, I was still worried and I had good reason to be.

Later on the same day, after Red and Maguire had headed west, I met up with Richard Tyrrell, my most able captain. We discussed the new developments and agreed that the favourite options for the third prong was either via the wave or up through the midlands.

'So, Hugh,' he said once our discussion seemed to reach a conclusion, 'what is it you want me to do?'

'I want you to take a pre-emptive strike. It may amount to nought, but I want you to take a force into Westmeath and await the third prong.'

'So you think the midlands is the favourite option?'

'Yes, I do. Also, a landing could happen anywhere on the coast. Where would I put you? I'm willing to take a gamble on Westmeath.'

'Why?'

'Well, if it doesn't materialise, you are close enough to either the Blackwater or Ballyshannon to go and assist, should the need arise. And if the third prong does come through the midlands, I will know that my most able commander has studied the land for weeks and is in control of the situation. I also know that you will keep me informed.'

'There's no need for the flattery, Hugh,' he said smiling. 'But I think you are right. I'll go and make ready.'

As I watched Richard disappear into the distance, I thought of the feast the previous evening; of how the new developments were received; of how Red, Maguire and Richard had responded that morning; of all that we had been through already; and of how the situation had escalated. And I realised how far we had come. We were beginning to show real signs of unity, and nobody was flinching, as the stakes grew higher.

Chapter XX
A GREATER TEST

Burgh launched his plan in July. I was proved right when he attacked with three prongs, and, thankfully, the third force was also a land-based attack. As soon as I found out I sent word out across the province. However, even though we were as prepared as we could possibly be, not everything went according to plan and much worked against us. It had been a long time since I had served with Clifford, and even though I knew he was a formidable foe back then, he had grown and learned much since and proved to be far more dangerous than even I had contemplated. In the two months between his appointment and the combined attack, he set about quenching Connaught's fire with great gusto. As anticipated, he won some over with his charm and just ways, and without siding with the English many in Connaught abstained from supporting us. Others who refused to toe the line were harassed and persecuted by an energetic English force. Red and Maguire did their best to provide support but Clifford did not yield in his intensity one iota. It was a difficult time for the people of Connaught. However, through all their pain and suffering we managed to maintain a number of lords in rebellion and a sizeable force in the province.

In the meantime, Burgh was making preparations in the Pale and was proving to be an organised and efficient leader. He was only in office for two months before he launched his assault with an army double in size of any we had faced previously. And if their spirit could be measured, I would suggest it had multiplied tenfold. Burgh was truly a leader of men.

And when they attacked in July, it was so well orchestrated and synchronised, that it was like three parts of one body moving in unison.

Clifford approached the Erne from the south and met Red on

the north. Apparently, such was the charm of the man, Clifford smiled at Red and bowed respectfully. Red reciprocated and there was much laughter and cheering and jeering on both banks. For a full day Red provided Clifford's reflection on the opposite side of the river as Clifford moved east to probe for weaknesses.

However, Clifford then produced a strategic masterstroke. Both he and Red knew that Clifford could not afford any significant delay as the state of Connaught and shortage of food had slowed his progress by a few days already. Also, as his primary target was Ballyshannon, he could not afford to lose resources in any engagement short of his quarry. So, he gathered his army and made it look as though he was going to attempt a crossing and drive through Red's forces. Red took the bait and gathered all his forces together. Unbeknownst to Red, however, Clifford had sent Sir Calisthenes Brooke about five miles downstream to Belleek.

In the meantime, Burgh had marched from the Pale to Newry by the 12 July and on to the Blackwater Fort in a further two days. I knew of this march long before we saw the enemy at our door, thanks to my spies. But this Burgh is a wily rascal and I received no warning of an impromptu raid just before his main drive. In the panic, which ensued, I managed to lose my horse and my hat but nothing else. But I gained far more – a valuable lesson. After my words of advice to Red and Maguire, it was flagrantly foolish of me to allow my guard to drop so drastically. I got away with it this time but I could ill afford a similar scare.

At least it had given me an indication of Burgh's capabilities. I withdrew my army beyond the Blackwater Fort into the dense forest and waited for him. I left only forty men in the fort with the orders to hold it for as long as possible and then retreat to the forest when it became an impossible task. I wanted to test Burgh. He arrived with three and a half thousand men and set about attacking the fort. I'm extremely proud to say that my force of the fort fought gallantly and broke the first assault with relative ease. It was clear to see that Burgh was infuriated. He waded into the river himself rallying and driving his troops, but to no avail. On the first day, our force repulsed each and every attack and showed for the first time that they could hold a position. However, there was only forty of them and the enemy stood three and a half thousand strong! As per my orders, the men had stood fast and tested the enemy's guile. There was no doubt of the enemy's strength but I wished to test Burgh's trickery. On this occasion he disappointed me. So, my troops withdrew and the majority reached the safety of our forest.

Burgh was obviously pleased with the capture of the fort, and so the next day he made to drive on after us. When he reached the forest and noted our craftwork, he clearly despaired of what to do, for he did nothing! It was obvious that he feared penetrating the forest for a number of reasons. First, he would not be able to keep his army together. Desertions and confusion would be inevitable and would become the order of the day. Second, he would be entering into territory and conditions chosen by us which were certainly not those favoured by any English fighting force. Third, it would leave the Pale and Dublin wide open and undefended.

So he sat there. I watched and listened as messengers went to and fro. My spies informed me that both Burgh and the government were frustrated by the lack of progress. They both dearly wanted to deliver results but realised the risk of venturing into the forest where they would fall foul of disease and hunger, let alone the Irish arch traitor. Burgh corresponded with the government daily and still nothing happened. All we could do was wait. The ball was firmly in his court. So we waited.

Brooke crossed the Erne during the night and Clifford moved under dark an hour before dawn. Red followed on the north side of the river as quickly as he could but the bend in the river meant that he had a further distance to travel and Clifford was able to get his whole army across safely. Red cursed himself for this turn of events but, in fairness, it was a brilliant manoeuvre by Clifford.

However, Clifford knew that he was already short on time and didn't tarry on his laurels. As soon as he was sure all his men were across, he regrouped with great haste and set his sights on Ballyshannon. Red retreated in order to defend the castle and Maguire moved up to join him with O'Rourke.

The next day the ship Clifford was awaiting sailed up the river and delivered two cannons, which were set on the castle. Fierce fighting followed over the next two days without Red and Maguire making much of a dent in the English forces, though they were grinding on to the castle. I was incredibly pleased to hear that Red and Hugh heeded my advice and kept their cool. Well, they kept their cool until the fourth day of fighting. This was after Clifford moved a seven-hundred strong body of men up to the garrison, and Maguire and O'Rourke felt that they had to do something. They attacked in numbers to no avail and were eventually driven off easily by the English. Clifford could smell victory in the air. He knew that our forces were at a loss as to what to do, so he waited for them to make their next mistake.

The situation was now on a knife-edge. Clifford was pushing Red and Maguire back in the west and was about to take Ballyshannon. Burgh had the Blackwater under control and was trying to gain entry to our lands in the east. While to the south we received word that Lord Trimleston was advancing through the midlands. If Trimleston managed to defeat or get past Tyrrell, our position would become precarious indeed. The last thing we needed was an English force popping up between Red and myself.

I need not have worried. Captain Richard Tyrrell is a magnificent officer and he made light work of Trimleston. In Tyrrell's own words, once we met up after the battle: 'It was almost too easy, Hugh. We lay in wait for them in a narrow valley and they just strolled in. It was a veritable slaughter.'

News of the Battle of Tyrrell's Pass, as it became known, did not take long to filter through to Burgh and the government. Almost immediately Burgh drew back to Newry and the threat in the east was also vanquished almost as easily as the threat from the south. Now it just left Clifford in the west. Knowing that Ballyshannon was on the brink of collapse, I sent a messenger at once to Red informing him of Tyrrell's victory and Burgh's retreat. I told him I was breaking camp and moving to support him at Ballyshannon and that I would be there within two days. I practically begged Red and Maguire to just hang on as long as possible and not to do anything rash. However, I think I underestimated Red's ability and possibly even Maguire's. They managed to conjure up something between them, which was far better than just hanging on.

On the morning of the fifth day of the siege, Clifford was not attacked. Instead, about mid-morning a great cacophony of cheering and shouting could be heard to the south. Maguire and O'Rourke had wheeled around a great arc out of sight of the enemy and crossed the Erne. Now Clifford had O'Donnell at Ballyshannon, and Maguire and O'Rourke in the path of any retreat. He was running low on food and ammunition and he feared that new developments had come into play. However, Clifford was one of those remarkable men who can label himself a brave and dedicated soldier without a doubt in his heart. He stood fast and waited for confirmation of Burgh's failure to get past me from a reliable source. He surely would not trust the wild cheering and jeering from the troops of Maguire and O'Rourke.

'I tell you, Hugh,' said Red to me afterwards, 'I have never faced a man like that before. Balls of granite, he has. It was an honour to fight against him. A genuine hero.'

Once Clifford had his worst fears confirmed, he began his retreat. His march was ordered and dignified and he even refused to march at night so as not to give us the satisfaction. As a result it was a slow process – the nearest town big enough to provide protection and victuals was sixty miles away.

'My lad,' began Red as he gave me his account of the proceedings afterwards, 'told me that Clifford had made a speech early that morning. It appeared to be a great rallying battle cry and oozed confidence into his forces.'

Soon after we could hear the beat of the drums in the distance, which almost seemed to bellow: 'If we are to retreat, then by God we will do it with pride!'

I attacked almost immediately. It was savage, Hugh. The man kept a strict, tight line and not once did a solitary soldier among them break ranks. Sure they shot back at us and when we got in close, defended themselves, but they never broke from marching even though they saw comrade after comrade fall. The wounded, they picked up and carried, the dead they stepped over. After six hours they must have marched not more than ten miles and still the drums beat on relentlessly and their colours flew in the breeze. They had long since ceased returning fire as they had run out of powder, yet they marched on and only got involved when we got in close.

Sure, I think the gods must have taken pity and smiled upon

Clifford then and tried to even up the odds. Didn't the very heavens open up and pour the Lord's holy bathtub down on top of us. It drenched our powder and quenched our fire, and so we were reduced to getting in close. I decided to rest my foot soldiers and just keep up the attack with the horse, which followed Clifford for another few miles. I'd say he must have made fifteen miles that day, no more. The men called the battle Casan na gCuradh – The Ford of the Heroes – and they were. We did everything in our power to obliterate them but even though we inflicted a defeat on them, they managed to save the force from complete decimation.

.

Chapter XXI
THE POISONED CHALICE

After our respective victories at the Ford of the Heroes, Tyrrell's Pass and the Blackwater in July, it all went a bit quiet for the next few months. Elizabeth was furious and puzzled by her representatives' lack of progress. Countless letters and correspondence between herself and Dublin did little to quell her ire.

For my part, I was quite happy with our situation. The enemy still refused to acknowledge the threat we posed to their superiority and thereby refused to spend the necessary money, time and resource in tackling an increasingly painful boil that festered and grew on its neck. And this meant that we could sleep in peace. Our morale could not have been higher after our magnificent victories and the gathering of a substantial harvest. And we seemed to grow more united by the day.

Indeed, if there was any aspect of our position, which was disheartening, it was the inaction of the Spanish. We knew their intent was there – sure, had they not already sent two fleets that, unfortunately, never saw sight of Ireland? But it just seemed that we could not make any real progress without them and the war would inevitably follow the repetitive pattern of an English attack being repulsed, or an English relief column being ambushed by us. The men were not stupid and they would eventually tire of the futility of this existence. We would go on making progress and continue to erode their administration by convincing more Irish to join the revolt. But until the Spanish arrived on the scene that is all we could do. And even though I used time to my advantage, it was a finite resource and I could not continue to abuse it indefinitely. I was slightly worried that I needed to speed things up. However, I was certainly not as worried as the English.

And so in October I expected a relief column to once more

make for Monaghan. And I was not disappointed. That old warhorse, Burgh, led the expedition himself and I was ready. We hassled and harried the column and forced them to waste half of the powder and shot meant for the fort. They must have felt like they were trying to shoot ghosts. But that's by the by. The small victory we gained here was insubstantial compared to the Biscuits or Clontibret or a score of others.

The real victory came our way when Burgh retired to Newry as he was taken ill. It was but a few days into the expedition and his force still made on for Monaghan without him. Soon news of this bizarre turn had reached the ears of all the men and they were both curious and perplexed at his course of action. I allowed myself to smile.

A couple of days later we learned that Burgh had died of typhus. I cared not. I had sent an assassin to poison the cold-hearted son of a whore, and I would make it known far and wide that he had succeeded. I had no proof either way. But if people start talking about poison, then all of a sudden it becomes fact. Maybe my assassin was successful, maybe not. Maybe the typhus took him, maybe not. Either way, the enemy would know that we could get to them and that is a scary prospect. Suddenly, the colonist looks over his shoulder at every turn and mistrusts everything he eats.

I was enjoying my moment. And this was *my* moment. The enemy had been repulsed like we were swatting flies. The whole world knew we were in a good defensive position. We were, on the whole, winning the war. And their leader was now dead. The English Army lay in tatters and the Pale lay more open to me than a whore's legs. All I had to do was thrust.

And so why did I tarry? Why wait? Why not take advantage of a God-given opportunity? Because I had a brain in my head, that's why. Yes, I was advised, encouraged, baited, bullied and pushed into storming the Pale and I resisted every call. And why? Because I knew that no matter how much havoc we wreaked, how much damage we caused, how much progress we made, it would be but a futile gesture. For the English still controlled the wave, and as long as they did, they could reverse our fortunes at the snap of a finger. We needed Spain. How many times did I have to say it?

In the meantime, Lord Loftus and Lord Gardiner were put in temporary charge and Ormonde was sent to parley with me, which I was happy to do. I had long been a friend of Lord Ormonde's and I would hear what he had to say. Do not misunderstand me, I was still as resolute in my aims as ever, but I was intrigued to hear if their terms were changing in light of recent events.

Ormonde wanted us to meet and parley in Dundalk but I refused point-blank to enter the town. Instead, the negotiations took place in an open field not far from Dundalk. On the first day Ormonde arrived with his entourage and all were, as agreed, armed only with swords. Not one of us held any other weapon. However, where my army was visible across the hills, Ormonde had not brought any force with him. I wondered about this and thought that perhaps in spite of the war and everything that had happened, they still considered me a gentleman and felt I would honour my word – which I would – and that they were not in danger of harm or kidnap. I later learned from a source in the town that this was not the case. Ormonde had kept his army hidden in Dundalk for shame. Yes, for shame! Apparently, there has never before been a shabbier, rowdy, ill kempt and ill-disciplined shower of rogues to serve the Crown and Ormonde knew it.

However, it mattered not. I knew already that they were no match for my army and that I could destroy them at will and march on Dublin. But, as I have said before, that was not in my best interests at the moment. And so we talked.

'My Lord Tyrone,' greeted Ormonde.

'My Lord Ormonde,' I returned.

'Let us allow common sense to prevail and let us put an end to this tragedy this day, my Lord,' he began.

'Under what terms?' I retorted.

His face took on that expression of shock you see when one gets bitten by a rabbit, for one does not expect such a sweet-looking creature capable of such viciousness. So he recoiled at my tone, which may have been a touch arrogant.

'My Lord Tyrone,' he began again, 'Her Majesty merely wants you and your followers to return to her protective and loving bosom.'

'Hah!' I snapped. 'There's more love and care in a snake! Aye, and I would certainly feel more protected by a snake!'

He was visibly reeling. This was the last thing he expected.

'My Lord, how can you say such things after Her Majesty gave you everything you have—'

'Everything?' I demanded curtly.

'Why, yes, my Lord, everything: land, title, wealth beyond your wildest imagination—'

'Then you have very little imagination!' I retorted. 'My Lord Ormonde, you live like a child in a dream world. Her Majesty gave me nothing that was not mine already and she has taken far more than that! Were the O'Neills not once kings of Ireland? Did we not rule all? Did we not own the north? Aye, we did all those things and the English have eroded at them and taken what they could these past years. My father and generations of O'Neills before him have suffered indignity upon indignity at the hands of the English. And when my father was killed, I was put under the 'protection' of the Crown and all our possessions and lands were seized. And so when she made me Baron of Dungannon, I received but a fraction of my rights, and even when I became Earl of Tyrone, I received but a fraction more. And all the while Tirleach Luineach receives patronage from the Crown. Well, I grew weary of waiting for what was mine to come my way and so I will take it as the English took it from me. No, I owe nothing to the Queen but my vengeance. And by this cross on my sword, she will feast on a bountiful harvest of bitter vengeance.

'My Lord Tyrone—' began Ormonde again but I cut him off.

'O'Neill, sir!' I snapped. 'I am O'Neill! And I will have the birthrights of the O'Neill!' And having said my piece, I turned my horse and rode away, leaving my Lord Ormonde with much food for thought.

The next day we met again and I maintained my arrogant stance but I was ready to at least listen to the enemy's terms and deliver my own. And so once again we reached agreement. And yet again it was a completely false truce. Both sides would ultimately tire of these games, but for now they were necessary.

Chapter XXII
YELLOW FORD –1598

They truly are a two-faced bunch of bastards! Even though I know what to expect from them, I am still amazed at their arrogance and double standards. They accuse me of underhanded dealings as though butter would not melt in their mouths, yet I had reliable information that months before the end of the truce they were recruiting men for a sea expedition to the north, probably at Lough Foyle. Once again the truce was merely used by both sides to gather and prepare themselves for the inevitable hostilities to come. But I was not going to wait for them to arrive at my back door, so I decided to take pre-emptive action. As soon as the truce elapsed and negotiations broke down, I surrounded the Blackwater Fort. This eyesore had been an open wound on my border for too long and this time I was determined to be rid of it forever. However, even though the fort was a thorn in my side, it never once yielded the English access to Tyrone, but merely stood sentinel on the border. So to rid the Earth of this monstrosity was a secondary motive to me. My primary aim was to divert the attention of the enemy away from its sea invasion and bring its focus back to its existing land establishments.

Our forces surrounding the fort numbered just over four and a half thousand men as Red, Maguire and a great many others joined me in the siege. I felt it was time for something big to happen. We needed to kick the land awake and make the rest of the world really sit up and take notice.

Obviously, I soon became privy to much correspondence between the Crown and the council in Dublin. Surprise, surprise, there was much talk of sending a relief column. However, there was a feeling that they should not abandon the sea expedition, which gave me cause for concern. But there was one voice, which was coming across louder than any of the others – only because he was shouting you understand – and that was the voice of Henry Bagenal. He was absolutely enraged that they were still considering the sea expedition while their garrison at the Blackwater Fort fed themselves on their draught horses and grass. Good old Bagenal! I could always rely on the great buffoon to allow his personal vendetta against me to cloud his judgement. He was offering, no, he was insisting on raising an army and leading the relief column through the rebels himself. Soon enough the council gave into his demands, probably for a bit of peace and quiet, and postponed the sea voyage to the north in favour of relieving the Blackwater Fort. This decision was made at the end of July and I knew that Bagenal would not tarry once he had the authority to move against me. Thankfully, Red, Maguire, O'Rourke, MacMahon, Burke and a number of others were close enough at hand that we were meeting on a daily basis to monitor progress.

'And so, gentlemen,' I said once I had told them of Bagenal's relief column, 'it is time for us to prepare the land to welcome my dear brother-in-law.'

'But, sure, the ground is very boggy and open in the immediate vicinity of the fort itself, O'Neill,' said Maguire.

'That's very true,' concurred Red. 'It will be very difficult to lay in wait anywhere close to the fort.'

'Unless we lie in wait in Tyrone itself,' said Cormac. 'But, sure, that defeats the whole object of the exercise if we lie in wait beyond the fort.'

'We could always anticipate their route to the fort and pitch our ambush earlier than they would expect, for, make no mistake about it, expect it they will,' added Richard.

'Well, they should expect it by now,' said Maguire. 'After all, 'tis what we do best.'

'Gentlemen, if you please,' I interjected. 'I do have a plan if you would like me to outline it for you.'

This was met with the usual, jovial, sarcastic comments.

'However,' I continued, 'before I begin with my plan, I must inform you that I think we may need more men.'

'More?' came the incredulous cry from all quarters.

'Aye, more,' I returned calmly. 'Marshal Bagenal is mustering quite a force for himself. Bigger than any we have faced previously, and I want to destroy it and humiliate the English so that they can no longer view this conflict as an irritant, which will go away in due course. I want them to take this war as seriously as any war they are faced with on the continent. Also, I believe that when we reduce their current army to a laughing stock, that Spain and the rest of Ireland will hasten to our side in an instant. We have had enough half-hearted promises from these quarters. Now we must force them to take action.'

'How big is Bagenal's Army?' asked Richard.

'And how many more men do we need?' asked Red.

'Bagenal's force falls slightly shy of four and a half thousand men,' I replied to the first question, which brought forth a few whistles and sighs and, 'oh my dear Lords.'

'We already number four and a half thousand men,' I continued, 'so I think another few hundred, maybe a thousand men will guarantee victory.'

'Are you insane?' bellowed Maguire. 'If we are to take on an English Army of four and a half thousand men, then we must have at least fifty per cent more than them, O'Neill.'

'I think not,' I replied.

General murmuring suggested that, in the main, initial feelings sided with Maguire.

'I will endeavour to explain why I think but a few hundred extra will suffice in my plan, but before I do that, I want to know that we can raise those few hundred within a week.'

'Well, I could certainly muster one hundred and fifty, possibly two hundred with relative ease,' said Maguire.

'I too could gather two hundred,' said Red. 'But I would need to do it now to get them here from Tir Connell in time. But you must also surely be able to lay your own hands on some more men, Hugh.'

'Aye, I believe that I can get at least three hundred men, so we have no fears there. I would like to get another thousand altogether, so I would urge all of you to try and get some more men here within a week.' They all seemed relatively confident that they could do this with ease and that put my mind at rest. I was using this as a test to see how much strength we could call upon should the need arise in the future, and I was truly heartened by the response.

'Not a problem, Hugh,' said Red. 'Now tell us your master plan.'

'Essentially, gentlemen, the plan is to split Bagenal's force and destroy the two halves separately. The point at which we split his army is the Yellow Ford on the Callan River. It is the only point he must pass on his march and that is where we will strike to telling effect. He will certainly not use the main road from Newry to get to the Blackwater, but there is no way he can avoid leading an army of that size over the Callan River anywhere other than the Yellow Ford. It's the only feasible pass, and from there he will need to get over the hill between the river and the fort and down through the bog.

'Also, I intend to cut a trench in that bog about halfway between the hill and the fort. This trench will need to be at least five feet deep and a mile long so that we can get enough men in there comfortably and well hidden. We will also plash the forests on his route and build some spiked elephant traps around the country so that we can encourage him to use the correct channel.

'We will, of course, indulge in some sniper fire almost as soon as he leaves Newry in an effort to guide him down the right road. However, as soon as we clap eyes on him as we lay in wait near the river, we will attack in great strength and drive him through the passage we want him to take. Oh yes, when he is close enough, we will let him know our strength and dictate the fight.'

'Will that not be a bit dangerous considering the size of his force?' asked Maguire. 'The last thing we want, after all, you have said this yourself on a number of occasions, is to fall into open battle with the English.'

'That will not happen because the English will be marching in column which will mean they won't have time to organise for battle. Also, the country is not ideal for open battle. And finally, their main objective is to relieve the garrison at the Blackwater, not to fight us.'

I allowed this to be digested before I continued.

'They will also be laden down with provisions for the fort, so we will watch for an ideal opportunity and have a special squad on standby at the Yellow Ford so that they can cause a bit of carnage and make it impassable, thereby splitting their army.'

Once again I allowed this idea to penetrate the grey matter.

'It all sounds very simple and easy to execute, Hugh,' began Red. 'But you know yourself that it is very often an entirely different proposition in practice.'

'I am well aware of it,' I said evenly. 'Which is why we must keep each other clearly informed throughout the battle. Each man must be crystal clear on his responsibilities and each officer must be fully conversant with the overall battle plan. If we cannot drive them to the Yellow Ford, then we must abandon the plan and retreat to Tyrone. If other aspects of the plan are not going according to our preparations, then we must take a view at the time.'

'Like what, for example?' demanded Maguire.

'Like if Bagenal decides that his priority is to engage in a fight and not move on to the Blackwater, then we must decide quickly whether we want to get involved or not. Like I have already said, the country does not suit open battle, so if he wants to fight, the advantages will still lie with us. But it will really depend on how things are going at the time. I refuse to risk our men in a hideous defeat if all we need to do is retreat and wait for another day.'

'And what happens if we call it wrong at the time and we end up with a hideous defeat anyway?' challenged Maguire.

'When I say we take a view at the time, I mean we look at the entire situation, and if we are confident of delivering a crushing blow to the Crown, we continue. However, anything less and we desist.'

Silence fell for a few moments before I continued.

'I would be incredibly suspicious and unconvinced if you did not question the plan and blindly went along with it. But I cannot help feeling that you do not share my confidence.'

'I have already said, Hugh,' responded Red, 'that it all seems to work nicely but it is just the size of Bagenal's force that worries me.'

'Aye,' ranted Maguire, 'that bothers me and the fact that you dismiss it so nonchalantly, O'Neill, and expect us to annihilate an English Army with but a small numerical advantage! That part of the plan smacks of lunacy to me. It scares me. You are normally Mister Cautious, Mister Prudent. You are a perfectionist – everybody recognises, hates and admires it as a quality in equal measure. Yet, here you are, dismissing the English Army as though we might brush them away like children flinging stones. I don't know, sometimes I think you are two people, O'Neill, and it confuses the hell out of me.'

'Maybe,' said Red once Maguire had finished his rant, 'Hugh is hiding something from us just as he did when he went to Dublin after the Biscuits. And, let's face it, there are without a doubt numerous other examples of when he has held something back from us.'

'Aye,' agreed Maguire, 'that's true enough.'

I allowed a smile to flicker momentarily across my lips – just long enough for it to register in the mind's eye before I pulled my poker face and gave assurances that nothing could be further from the truth.

'I think it is a great plan,' said Richard. 'I see no flaw in it and I believe we can do it quite easily with five to five and a half thousand men. But there's the problem: it is the biggest challenge we will have faced so far, gentlemen, and so naturally we begin to doubt ourselves and look for the flaw in the plan. "Surely," we think in our heads, "it cannot be this simple to defeat the English?" And so doubt creeps in and haunts us. But it is that simple, gentlemen. And we must believe it is that simple. And we must convince the men that it is that simple. Very often the best plans are the most simple plans. We can do this. I have all the confidence in us but we must believe it ourselves.'

'Ach, even if we convince ourselves,' began Maguire, 'we will never convince four and a half thousand Irishmen that we can do it.'

'So why did we bother to begin the rebellion?' I demanded.

'Ach, you know well why,' dismissed Maguire.

'Yes, I know why, but I want you to tell me why, Maguire.'

He just glared at me, so I launched into a spiel.

'Yes, gentlemen, we all know why we got involved in this rebellion. We had had enough of the English injustice, bullying, theft, murder and other crimes. We were angry and we wanted to vent our spleen. We wanted to take back what was rightfully ours. But deep down it was more selfish than that: it was greed. We wanted more land, more property, more wealth, more title, more power… just more. But it has moved on since we started it. There's a different feeling: something else to fight for. It's something you cannot measure, something intangible. It is the Irish nation, gentlemen. Yes, that pride and unity you feel coursing through your heart is the pulse of the nation. And it's growing. You cannot understand why it holds your attention and mesmerises you in such a fashion. I don't know either, but I would imagine that it has something to do with the fact that it separates us from the English. It differentiates us from everyone else. It binds us together. It makes us Irish. Just as the English, French, Spanish, Dutch and every other member of a nation can identify with one another, so we are beginning to do the same. And it feels good. No, we may not gain materially from defending and fighting for this honour, but it is worth much more than any money could ever buy. That is why we must take on the English Empire and we can defeat it. We knew from day one that the stakes would escalate, as the war grew ever longer. And that was when we were merely feathering our own nests. We knew that we would eventually face an army the size of Bagenal's and greater but it did not deter us. And we must not allow it to deter us now. We have a far greater prize to fight for now and that is why we are suddenly nervous. We must strengthen our resolve and fight for our country, our nation.'

'You are right,' said Red nodding. 'Of course, you are right. We knew we were taking on the English Empire. The conflict was never going to remain at the initial levels and I would wager that if we succeed—'

'When,' I interjected.

'Correction noted,' said Red. '*When* we succeed in this battle, the English will hit us with all they have got in an effort to gain vengeance. But we will match and better them. Hugh is right. We *must* win this battle and we *will* win this battle!'

It seemed that everybody was injected with a new-found buoyancy after that. Determination and belief buzzed through the air and it would filter through to the troops in due course.

The next week was spent preparing the land. We dug our trench and elephant traps. We weaved our magic in the woods. And we took the men through the overall plan and their individual specific roles in fine detail until there could be no doubt of what was expected. Everyone was ready.

Bagenal moved towards the Blackwater on the morning of the 14 August and marched approximately a mile from the main road in a parallel line. Our snipers started stinging their flanks like wasps almost immediately and after a while there was the occasional disappearance as the elephant traps devoured victims.

However, the real affair began late in the morning when I led an attack on Bagenal's van. To my eternal joy I saw that he had split his force with two regiments in the van and two in the main. I could not see the rear of his line from where I was, but I suspected, correctly as it transpired, that there were also two regiments in the rear. He had also left a sizeable gap between the sections, which enabled us to get between them. So, while I set about attacking the van, Red simultaneously attacked the rear with the object of pinning them down and isolating them from the main army. In the meantime, I drove the van led by Colonel Richard Percy towards the Yellow Ford.

He sped his force across the ford and up and over the hill. From there he could see the fort, and the garrison within its walls could see him. At this point a huge cheer went up from the fort and also from Percy's column, which gathered pace and stormed onwards even though they were suffering losses on both flanks from my men. All of a sudden the ambush drew off and Percy must have thought he had got through to the fort. Then just as suddenly fire opened up from the hidden trench in front of them. At this stage they were beginning to lose shape and gaps were appearing all through their line. But they steeled their resolve and charged the trench and broke past it but with great loss. Surely, they were safe and sound now! But no! Richard Tyrrell, who had been monitoring the situation and waiting for them to breach the trench, suddenly burst from nowhere with my cavalry and cut the remnants of Percy's regiment to pieces.

One regiment down, five to go.

Regiment number two had passed the Yellow Ford and was receiving similar treatment to its predecessor when Bagenal arrived from the middle section. However, before he could issue a single command, he was shot through the head and killed. The bastard of a brother-in-law I loathed was no more. In but a fleeting instant my nemesis, my tormentor, my despised adversary was removed from my life. From a purely selfish perspective I was delighted, but more significant to our chances of success that day was that the leader of the enemy force was dead. At this point Wingfield assumed command and ordered a retreat.

However, this was easier said than done as my special task force had already done its job. Oxen lay hamstrung and screaming in the ford with their wagons capsized and their loads scattered effectively blocking the route of retreat. This left the middle third and fourth regiments split on either side of the Callan. But Wingfield is a magnificent leader. He quickly decided to cut his losses and so abandoned the provisions and ordered the oxen to be killed. Then he would speed to the fifth and sixth regiments who were pinned down by Red.

I saw a fantastic opportunity at this juncture and I took it. I ordered the men from the trench to move out and make for the river. Thankfully, an English captain named Henry Cosby saw this manoeuvre and took the bait. In Wingfield's absence he ordered his regiment to attack in order to break through and get to the fort. As soon as they were clear of the river, we blocked their retreat and I sent the cavalry in after them whilst the trench men returned to their trench. In but a few minutes his regiment was a disorganised rabble in extreme trouble. Wingfield had, by this time, managed to consolidate his final two regiments and send them on an orderly retreat to a nearby hill, which they would hold until the rest of the column was clear of the battlefield. Imagine his dismay when he turned towards the Yellow Ford once more only to find Cosby off on his heroics and in difficulties. His next move would prove critical, and I watched him as he considered his limited options. Regiments one and two lay in tatters with but a few souls remaining on the far side of the river. The third regiment had followed Cosby across without Wingfield's authority to meet a similar fate. The fourth was gradually being destroyed at the Yellow Ford as it tried to clear and hold the pass open for their retreat. And he had just ordered the fifth and sixth to secure a hill so that the force, or what was left of it, might secure a safe passage to Armagh. So there really was not much choice. Either he sacrificed those across the river and withdrew the rest in an effort to try and salvage at least part of the army, or he must send a force to assist the retreat across the river. The first option would obviously involve heavy losses in a sacrificial move unless by some miracle they managed to fight their way out on their own. The second option, however, was a more noble effort but could mean ultimate annihilation for the whole army. Which is why I was incredibly surprised that he went for it.

Wingfield sent the fifth regiment to the aid of the stupid Cosby, and by the time they got there, I'm certain Wingfield bitterly regretted his decision to send them. The third were all but destroyed — a handful of survivors at best. All the while their fourth regiment was being pummelled whilst trying to hold the pass open. Also, when the fifth went off to try and rescue the third, Red piled the pressure on the sixth and severely diminished their numbers. Indeed, if the retreat from the ford had been delayed by another half an hour, there would have been a real doubt whether they would have had a route to take as Red was making such progress. But somehow some of them did manage to escape and they retreated to Armagh Cathedral to lick their wounds. It must have been a terrifying night for them as they sat there surrounded by our campfires on the hills. They must have believed that come the morning we would send them to hell where they would be reunited with their comrades. There was less than a quarter of their force remaining and many of those were wounded. But even at their fittest and strongest they were no match for us.

My troops were magnificent. Patience, discipline and skill won the day for us as we went about the battle without deviating from our tactics in the slightest. From very early on in the day it was obvious for all to see that the English were anxious, frustrated, frightened, worried and clueless. They ran out of ideas early on and never really regrouped. It was clear from the outset that there was virtually no leadership and that very soon the enemy had lost the little respect it had held for their commanders.

I had never previously witnessed an English force so disorganised and scared. Long before the end of the battle, they had abandoned all hope of victory and even surviving to see another day. It was real fear and it was easy to understand why. This was the largest English force assembled in all of Ireland and they were trapped. They couldn't escape to spread word of their plight and even if they could, who would come to their aid? There was no other sizeable assembly of English soldiers in the country. If they were to rely on reinforcements from England, it would take weeks for them to arrive. They were on their own and they knew it. Their superior weapons brought them no advantage in these conditions and they knew it. They were outnumbered and they knew it. And they were at our mercy and they knew it. Yes, it was real fear. A fear I have never witnessed in an English force before or since and it boosted my men with the unshakeable conviction that we could and would win this war.

At the end of the day the English suffered over three thousand casualties. Their main force in Ireland was destroyed having lost several colours and regiments. The Blackwater Fort was besieged with no immediate reprieve in sight. Indeed, the most disastrous statistic of the battle as far as the English were concerned was that we had captured all the victuals and ammunition for the relief of the fort. It transpired that they had provisions to survive for just over a week, which enabled us to capture the stronghold with relative ease.

The Battle of the Yellow Ford has subsequently been analysed as the greatest victory sustained by Irish forces over the English in the long and tiresome historic struggle. It was secured without too much effort and put the fear of God into the army of oppression. More than that, it gave rise to the theory, in both our men and those of the enemy that we knew our country and how to conduct battle in Ulster, and the English did not. In effect, the majority of men on both sides saw us as invincible.

I made sure that someone was allowed to escape to bring word of the battle to Dublin. It was not long before I received a snivelling, crawling letter from the council begging for the remainder of the army to be given safe passage. After all, they said, my enemy, Marshal Bagenal was now dead. I decided to comply with the request. I was not about to slaughter a thousand virtually defenceless men and fuel the ire and outrage of the Crown. I also set the terms of surrender and against much advice from my peers, I was very generous. I allowed the garrison at the Blackwater to join with the army at Armagh, but to leave behind their weapons, ammunition and colours. I then allowed the whole force to retire to Dundalk. I took the Blackwater and Armagh leaving the enemy with no base anywhere near my territory. The English nearly snapped off my arm accepting these conditions. My peers were furious initially. However, I had my reasons.

It was the end of August and the last thing we needed, even though we were more than able to cope, was a winter campaign. There was a harvest to be gathered, families to feed and wounds to tend and heal. Also, time spent not fighting would be time spent further reinforcing Ulster against reinvasion. We had won strategic locations such as the Blackwater Fort and now was the time to strengthen our defences.

Also the English are a mighty opponent and they would not take the rout at the Yellow Ford lying down. They would be back and they would be stronger than ever. We would need to strengthen our own forces if we were to see any more Yellow Fords. Emissaries were sent to the Desmonds, theThomonds, other Gaelic Lords and most importantly to Spain to beseech assistance. We launched a propaganda campaign second to none. Rumours ran rife regarding many of our victories especially the Yellow Ford. There were even stories of up to ten thousand English dead in the war so far and not one casualty on the Irish side at the Yellow Ford! However, the real fuel for our propaganda fire was provided by the English themselves. Many of those who were spared at the Yellow Ford returned home with stories of savage massacres, heroic Irish warrior giants, unspeakable, heinous acts and refused to return to that barbaric land.

The reasons for my leniency in settling the terms bore fruit almost immediately. The English arrived at the decision I had hoped for and postponed any further action until the spring instead of launching a reflex revenge campaign in the winter. Buoyed by our success, the men worked tirelessly through the winter months to ensure that when the enemy did return they would not be able to penetrate Ulster. A number of Irish lords, notably in Connaught, made moves to join the struggle once we resumed in the spring. Also, the Spanish were certainly warming to the proposition of assisting our cause. Certainly there was an ulterior motive to their support – that of using Ireland as a back door in their own conflict with England. But we needed their help and their ultimate aim was peripheral to securing this. And finally, the world was beginning to hear, through our elaborate propaganda campaign, of our magnificent, and sometimes-exaggerated successes.

All was going well.

Chapter XXIII
LOUGH FOYLE

We had destroyed the English Army and the Pale laid defenceless. There was but one thought in everyone's head: on to Dublin. That is, everyone except for me. I had my reasons and I knew it was right not to attack.

'What's this nonsense about not attacking the Pale?' demanded Maguire as he stormed into my quarters. 'It's the best shagging chance we are ever likely to get. Their army over here is beaten – you said that yourself. It lies in tatters a few miles yonder. They will send another for sure, but that will take months. What is going on in your head, O'Neill?'

'Hugh is right, Maguire,' said Red.

This took them aback somewhat. If they were expecting anyone to go for it now, it would have been Red.

'Now is not the time,' he continued.

'Not the fucking time?' raged Maguire. 'God blast it, man, when will be the time?'

'When Hugh decides,' replied Red.

Maguire and his cohorts looked stunned. I think they would have believed it more if Christ Himself had come in and sat down rather than what they were currently hearing.

'Listen to me for a moment, you two,' said Maguire. 'The English are beaten in Ireland. The Pale will never be easier to take. There is talk up and down the land that the country is joining us in revolt. If this mysterious Spaniard, Cobos, is to be believed, Spain is ready to assist our fight. Imagine the support we could muster if we take the Pale. Sure the Pope himself would come over and give us a hand. Every Catholic in Europe would probably believe that Hugh is Christ risen if we conquer the Pale. I'm telling you, we will never have a better chance, ever.'

'You may well be right, Maguire,' I said rising to my feet. 'But

I believe we will see a better chance. Quite soon, in fact.'

Everyone fell silent now, waiting to hear what was to be said.

'I received two pieces of news this day: one good and one bad. The good news is that the Spaniards have received the blessing of His Holiness, the Pope, and even now are recruiting men for the expedition. The bad news is that the English are sending a fleet to Lough Foyle in order to navigate the Bann and relieve the garrison at the Blackwater Fort. As a result of the latter news, I feel it would be foolish to drive on to Dublin when we will be needed here.'

At this point, I was surrounded by solemn faces.

'Once again, gentlemen, our lack of naval defences works against us. Once the Spanish fleet is involved, that particular problem will be eradicated. Until then we will defend Fortress Ulster and Castle Connaught and monitor the situation. If revolt spreads far and wide across the land, we may be able to change tactics.'

Chapter XXIV

THE NATION WAKES

If the effects after Clontibret and the Biscuits were remarkable, then the effects after the Yellow Ford were truly astounding. It seemed as if the whole world gasped. As the news broke, the entire country came to life and joined us in rebellion. It swept across the land like a wave taking everything with it in its path. It was as if the entire nation were sitting until the wonderful news reached them, and once they heard they stood upright and proud. At that very moment I believe the concept of the 'Irish nation' was born.

Through Laois and Offaly, from Dublin to Wexford and all of Munster rose and took action against their alien landlords. Raids became commonplace on the Pale and the old English of the towns kept themselves locked away from the fearful danger. Each day more estates were deserted as landlords fled their stolen homes. Within a few short days the whole Munster Plantation, which was conducted after the fall of the Earl of Desmond, was pulled asunder.

This was truly great news and it was now evident for all to see that we had made Ireland ungovernable for the English and that we now had our greatest chance to overthrow the colonists. However, the momentum needed to be maintained. I was still reluctant to strike at Dublin and the Pale in a full attack, as I remained uneasy about leaving Ulster defenceless. The expedition, which was due to land in Lough Foyle had been diverted to Dublin after news of the Yellow Ford reached them. But that did not mean that the English were incapable of raising another fleet for the north. But I had to do something or the momentum would be lost. So I decided to send a small group of commandoes to assist the rebellion down south. My ever faithful and diligent friend Captain Richard Tyrrell would lead Owney

O'Moore with a force of *bonachts* to Munster.

'Are you certain that Owney O'Moore will toe the disciplined line?' Richard asked when I told him my plan.

'O'Moore will cause you no problems,' I assured him. 'I will speak to him and ensure that he knows what is expected of him.'

'Well, Hugh, you know him better than I, but you can tell him from me that if he even comes close to putting one of the men's lives, let alone the mission, in jeopardy, that I will kill him there and then with my own hands.'

'O'Moore is eager to fight as are his men. But he wants to do it properly. He means to learn from our experiences. He is a good man and he will not let you down,' I replied.

'I don't doubt his intentions, Hugh. Nor do I doubt his intelligence and ability. I am merely concerned about his fiery temper and control.'

'There is no need to worry, Richard my friend,' I soothed putting my hand on his shoulder. 'I will speak to him and ensure he knows the importance of control, discipline and patience. I will also ensure he knows that if his life is sacred to him, then he had better not cross you.'

As Richard left me, I wondered whether I had made the right decision. Should I have cut to the jugular and made for the Pale? Should I have allowed Owney O'Moore to go with Tyrrell?

I truly did not know the answers. But there was one thing for certain – it would not be long before I would find out.

Chapter XXV

A NEW NEMESIS – 1599

Of course, in the meantime, the English would need a new leader, and so I heard of the appointment of yet another new Lord Deputy. I called a meeting to deliver the news.

'Gentlemen,' I began, 'the reason I assembled all of you here today is because I have some important news to impart. Elizabeth is sending Essex to take charge and she is providing him with the means to do it. He will lead an army of seventeen and a half thousand men and will also receive support from the English lords over here. Regular supply ships will be sent to Dublin carrying food, clothing, weapons and ammunition. In short, gentlemen, he will lead the largest and best-equipped army ever to set foot in Ireland. He will even, so rumour has it, be granted the exalted title of Lord Lieutenant instead of Lord Deputy.'

'You say "will", Hugh,' said Red. 'When will this be actioned if it has not already been?'

'Within the next few weeks,' I replied. 'It's not official, yet. Indeed, it has not really been decided yet, but it looks extremely likely. It appears that there are many at Court opposed to the idea. I will certainly endeavour to make that work in our favour.'

'But who is this Essex?' asked Cormac. 'Does anyone know anything about him?'

'Apart from his expedition to Cadiz and the Azores, you mean?' replied Maguire sarcastically.

'No,' responded Cormac. 'You know what I mean. He is very young and inexperienced, so why has Elizabeth picked him? It is one thing launching a surprise attack, it's another running a country and a major military campaign.'

'I know a little of the boy,' I replied. 'His name is Robert Devereux and he is currently Her Misery's favourite. He is her blue-eyed boy at the moment because of his handsome looks, dashing manner and never-ending charm. The boy must be Irish!'

This got a wee laugh and eased the tension somewhat. I waited for the few chuckles to subside before continuing.

'However, this is not the only reason he is her favourite. They say that he reminds her of her young love Dudley.'

'We can make that work for us,' said Red.

'Yes,' I replied, 'I intend to. Also, they say that he literally begged Elizabeth to be given Ireland to sort out for her. He has little military experience, although I believe he has had some training. To be honest, he has done nothing of note and precious little is known of him. In my mind, at the moment, our greatest weapons against him are the enemies he has made at Court through jealousy towards the young man. That combined with Elizabeth's blind affection for him and my old favourite, Time, will serve us well. Let my "contacts" at Court work their ways on those who oppose his appointment, and cause division and discontent in the Queen's own garden. And let's give Essex time and space. Let's see what he does with this considerable power at his disposal. In time we will be able to gauge the threat he poses.'

All heads were nodding in agreement.

'So,' began Maguire, 'I suppose we fortify our defences and continue to conduct the odd raid in the meantime?'

'That's our course,' I replied nodding.

'Well, that's simple enough,' said Red. 'But for now, let's sample some of that famous O'Neill hospitality. And I don't mean the kind Gavalach received!' Hugh Gavalach was a rival to the title of O'Neill who I had executed some years before.

With that we all retired to the hall for a feast in a much more relaxed mood.

So we took it relatively easy for a while. I kept an eye on young Devereux and waited for him to move. I watched and waited. And I watched and waited.

Chapter XXVI
ESSEX MOVES

It appears our lad was a touch hasty, let alone arrogant. In only two months he has managed to allocate his seventeen and a half thousand strong army in a manner, which not only provides the possibility but actually encourages desertion! He has managed to spread himself so thin that he cannot even quell the minor rebellions erupting around the country, let alone deal with the major conspirators. His force is spread so far and wide that he cannot afford, through time or money, to revictual them, so they starve. In only two months he has dispersed his army of seventeen and a half thousand men into a shambles of a few outposts. He has encouraged illness and desertion and demoralised his troops more than any defeat we have ever inflicted upon him. He has done more harm to the English cause without any serious action taking place these past couple of months than we have ever managed to achieve through four years of warfare. In fact, that gives me an idea. How would it seem to the English if Essex had ulterior motives? If, for example, he decided to throw in his lot with us, where would that leave us with the English? Where would it leave us with the Irish? And, probably most important of all, where would it leave us with the Spanish? Well, I'll certainly give that some thought, but I'll leave it to one side for the moment.

However, getting back to Essex, I must say that he has proved to be the most incapable commander so far amongst the English forces. Perhaps some of it was not of his own making and was down to the enemies he has at Court. We certainly tried and succeeded, through our agents at Court, to turn the tide against him. However, he certainly has not helped himself. My God, his tactics constitute madness itself! I cannot believe the man's naivety. He must know that he has enemies at Court, so why would he go about splitting his force in such a manner? The only one who will ever know will be Essex himself. Maybe I should ask him.

Essex has been foolish. Instead of striking at us in the north with his vast army, he chose to break it up and send parts of it through the country in order to quell the rebellion. He proved himself to be no more than a mere boy. I grew tired of waiting for him to do something and I was in the process of taking action against him when I received distressing news. King Philip II of Spain was dead and had been succeeded by his son Philip III. I knew that he was not as volatile as his father but I did not know whether he would support our cause or work towards peace. I was pondering the possibilities when Red arrived at Dungannon.

'Great news, Hugh,' he said as he burst into the hall. 'Sir Conyers Clifford no longer poses a threat to us. We set upon him in great numbers in the Curlieu Mountains and completely destroyed his force. After facing the wily old fox before, I gave him no chance to regroup on this occasion and did not stop until the collective English arse was red and bloody from the beating. Even better than that, Clifford himself, his colonel Sir Alexander Radcliffe and other influential officers were numbered among the hundreds of dead and doomed souls. A magnificent victory! If there was any doubt that Connaught was ours, that doubt has been successfully removed.'

'That is indeed fantastic news, Red,' I replied with much enthusiasm. 'That should give Her Majesty food for thought and serve to further delay any action by Essex. Now we can concentrate all our forces on the Pale and watch for Essex.'

'What do you think he will do?' asked Red.

'I'm not sure. I know he is being put under tremendous pressure from Court to take direct action against us. But he must know that it would be a futile gesture. From his great army of seventeen and a half thousand men I would be surprised if he could muster more than two thousand for the expedition. He has spread his forces far and wide and his army has vanished like the banshee with a new soul. His cause is lost and we have a great opportunity here and now to evict the colonists forever. If only Spain would come. We would end this war in an instant.'

'Speaking of which,' replied Red, 'what news from Cobos?'

I told him of the news of the king.

'That is indeed worrying news,' he replied. 'But did Alonso hint at any activity?'

'They are preparing. They are forever preparing. When are they going to act?'

'Hugh, I have been thinking about this and I am beginning to think that it is all false promises.'

'I believe Alonso to be genuine,' I replied, defending my friend.

'I don't doubt his intentions,' said Red, 'but I do doubt the motives of the new king. I am sure Philip II would always have tried to help. Sure didn't he send two fleets, which were beaten back only by the weather? But Philip III wants peace, I'm sure of it.'

'We all want peace,' I retorted.

'Yes, Hugh, but at what price? We have come too far to turn back now. We must have Spain with us or all is lost.'

'I know, Red,' I said resignedly. 'And I have a plan, but much relies on Essex. If only the bastard would move against us, then I could arrange a parley with him and hatch my plan.'

'And what is this great plan, may I ask?'

'I'm going to convince Essex to desert Elizabeth and side with us.'

This was met by a great belly laugh from Red, which rocked the very foundations of Dungannon.

'You cannot be serious, Hugh!' said Red wiping tears of laughter from his eyes. 'He will never be a traitor to the Queen he loves.'

'Oh, but I am serious, Red,' I replied. 'More serious than I have ever been about anything else in my whole life.'

'Come on now, Hugh,' said Red regaining a serious visage. 'A joke is a joke, but cop on to yourself now, man!'

'I am deadly serious, Red. Just think about it for a minute, will you? The wedge between Elizabeth and Essex is being hammered in so fast and they are being driven so far apart from each other that they are practically unrecognisable to each other. Essex has received orders not to return to England without permission. His enemies at Court already label him traitor and say that his tardiness and dispersing of his grand army are solely down to his sympathy and affection for me, the friend of his deceased father. He is without hope of victory against me – he must surely know this, and yet he will lose everything unless he achieves this victory. Also, it is known far and wide that he has designs on the English Crown for himself. I am sure I can convince him that his only option is to throw in his lot with us. And if he does, Phillip III will also join us.'

'And if he doesn't?' replied Red.

'I am sure I can at least achieve a parley with Essex and myself alone, and then it is really my word against his.'

'The way you tell it, Hugh, it certainly sounds feasible. But I'm not sure if you will be able to translate it into practice.'

'Red, my friend, rest assured that if I get my parley with Essex, there will soon after be much talk of Hugh O'Neill, King of Ireland and England.'

Chapter XXVII
SETTING THE TRAP

Essex was eventually forced to move against the north by Court as he had run out of excuses and options. This gave me the perfect opportunity to contact him and arrange a parley. I sent Henry O'Hagan to speak to Essex on my behalf with the instructions that the parley must be between just Essex and myself, and he agreed. We met on the Lagan River and I led my horse into the river and sat in the middle with the water lapping at my horse's belly. Essex stood on the bank alone. He had but a few in his entourage on the hill above and I had many hundreds fully armed on horseback watching the proceedings.

'My Lord Tyrone,' greeted Essex.

'My Lord Essex,' I replied.

'Many thanks for agreeing to this parley,' he said. 'I would dearly love to settle our differences with words and not war.'

'I too, my Lord,' I responded. 'But it has been made impossible for me to ignore the injustices. Believe me, I have tried reason on many occasions but to no avail. The cretins who reside in the Pale tell lies about me and whine to Her Majesty the Queen about the smallest of problems. They behave like snotty children and have no dignity.'

'I do appreciate your grievances, my Lord, truly I do. In my own short time in Ireland I have witnessed their foul and contemptible behaviour at first hand and I have informed Her Majesty accordingly. But we two have never talked of peace between us, so let us try to resolve the problems posed by and to both sides.'

'I would love nothing better, my Lord Essex, than to live by your side in perfect harmony with all Englishmen and under the protection of Her Majesty's wing. But I fear I cannot. I have been betrayed on more occasions than I care to remember, and I will not put myself and my people in that position again.'

'So what is it you desire, my Lord Tyrone?'

I issued my demands and Essex looked horrified.

'They are great demands indeed, my Lord. You know Her Majesty will grant some concessions but certainly not all.'

'Then take up your arms, Lord Essex, and try to defeat me.'

'I cannot, my Lord. In my heart I feel certain that we can reach an understanding and I refuse to return to war without attempting to resolve our differences.'

I sighed with resignation and stared at heaven momentarily as if in deep thought.

'Your father, Lord Essex,' I said, 'was a dear friend whom I loved with all my heart. For his memory I will hear what you have to say, my Lord.'

'Yes, my father always spoke highly of you, my Lord Tyrone, and he also loved you with all his heart. It would hurt his dearly departed soul more than anything else if we were pitted in a bloody struggle against one another.'

'Aye, 'tis true, my Lord Essex, and truly I wish to avoid hostilities, if possible. So go on, tell me what you have to say and let us see if it is acceptable.'

Essex delivered his terms, which had improved significantly since my truce with Wallop and Gardiner. However, they still fell some way short of my needs.

'Well, my Lord, my own demands and Her Majesty's remain some distance apart. Much of what you have just said is completely unacceptable to my mind. And I fail to see how we can make both ends meet.'

'I also see difficulties, my Lord, but we must try or all is lost.'

I could see in my heart he was full of despair and almost at his wits' end.

'I hear, my Lord Essex,' I said changing the subject, 'that your enemies at Court are many and conspire against you in your absence.'

His face changed and told me everything I needed to know.

'How would you know this, my Lord Tyrone?' he asked.

'You seem to forget, my Lord, that in all my many years of service to Her Majesty, I spent some time at Court and yet have many friends there. And enemies also,' I added. 'I know how the Court works and, believe me, your enemies spout lies about you in Her Majesty's ear every waking minute of every waking hour of every waking day. They make your task impossible and await the day when your failure will be complete. And believe me, you will fail. For you will never secure all your demands for peace with me. Do you truly believe that Her Majesty wants all of those demands honoured? Of course not! Her advisors at Court, your enemies, tell her that it would be shameful to accept anything less, knowing that you can never secure them. And should you resort to force I will have no alternative but to crush you. And crush you I will. Do not make me the instrument of your destruction, Lord Essex.'

'You underestimate me, sir! Why you do not even consider it an option that I might defeat you on the field of battle and bring your countrymen once more to their knees.'

'No, I do not, sir,' I returned simply.

'Why your arrogance is astounding, sir!' he raged.

'You, sir, confuse arrogance with confidence. You must realise that your weak rabble of an army is no match for mine. You will never be able to secure Ulster with it. Therefore, you cannot win a war against us. And even if a miracle should occur in your favour and you do manage to win, it will not receive its due credit at Court. Each and every one of your victories and successes thus far have been sneered at and dismissed as petty trifles at Court. You are in a no-win situation, and the longer it takes, the more damage your enemies do to you in your absence.'

'You talk gibberish, sir! And I will listen to no more!'

'Really?' I said as he turned to leave. 'So it is not true that Her Majesty stings your pride with insults such as suggesting that in two months you have not brought in one worthy rebel? Or, that I am able to sit at my leisure and laugh at your expense? Or, that I have been bragging of my victories on the continent? Or that your public marches in the south are quite ridiculous?'

'How could you possibly know these things?' he demanded.

'Like I said, my Lord, I have a great many powerful friends at Court and they are privy to the most confidential information. I dare say that the Queen herself would cease to breathe at the snap of my fingers.'

'I don't believe you!' he snorted.

'Really?'

'Yes, my Lord, I believe you to be a liar, a cheat and a scoundrel!'

'Oh stop, lad, you flatter me. Yes, I am all of those things and more besides. Quite a gentleman, in fact. I fancy, were it not for my present position on this side of the fence, I could fit in quite well at Her Majesty's Court.'

'My Lord Tyrone, I am disgusted that you would associate those foul qualities with any gentleman I know and I wonder that your boastful utterances are not merely hot air. If you had the power to have Her Majesty assassinated, you would have done so long ago,' he retorted with a smug grin which just begged to be punched.

But I delivered a blow far better than a punch. 'My dear boy, Essex,' I responded sighing resignedly, 'you are proving yourself to be more and more out of your depth here every time you open your mouth to speak. Do you know nothing of the game of politics that only gentlemen play? Are you really that naïve? Tell me, dear lad, why would I want to assassinate the Queen? I merely suggested that I had the power to do it. But what would happen then? A new king or queen would take the throne and the war would continue. And I would need to learn how to play against a new adversary. And who knows, the next monarch might not be such a penny-pinching skinflint and may actually provide the Lord Deputy with the money and resources to actually stand a chance in Ireland. And where would I be then? Hm? No, I'll not do the English that favour. Better to let the bald whore sit on the throne and become tired of me, I fancy.'

Essex was truly speechless. It was obvious that he was beginning to see that what I was saying was not only feasible but the only possible explanation. Before today he was a confused man, splashing around in his sea of troubles and not understanding any of it. Now it all made sense and he was more worried than ever before.

'My Lord Essex,' I resumed in a more soothing tone, 'I would advise you to go home and defend your honour against those who would destroy you in your absence. Look not to me for an enemy, for your true enemy is at your rear. However, I know as well as you do that Her Majesty has ordered you not to return until she commands it.'

Once again he looked at me in bewildered awe as if I were somehow reading his mind.

I merely shrugged. 'Now who do you suppose suggested that kind of an order to her?' I asked.

He looked at me in resignation.

'So you are trapped, my Lord. You cannot win in Ireland and you are unable to return unless you win. Your existence on earth is fast becoming a living hell.'

'What am I to do?' he practically begged.

'Well, I do have a proposition for you and it may sound completely insane at first, but I urge you to give it some thought before you make your decision.'

'Certainly,' he replied. 'What is it you propose, my Lord Tyrone?'

'Join me in rebellion and take the throne of England for your own.'

Chapter XXVIII

INVENTING THE STORY

I returned to my quarters directly after the meeting with Essex to find Red waiting for me.

'So,' began Red, 'do you think he will give it serious thought?'

'I'm not sure,' I replied. 'We have agreed a temporary truce which will give him time to think, but he remains loyal to Elizabeth even if the rumours that he wishes to succeed her as monarch are true.'

'So what do we do now?' asked Red.

'It's not up to us, my friend. The ball is in his court. It is his move. And his next move will give us a clear indication of what we must do. However, I would say that if King Phillip III were to hear of the rumours that Essex is to desert his queen and join forces with the Irish rebels, it might improve our chances of securing Spanish support sooner rather than later.'

I informed a few contacts of the possibility of Essex joining us and was very careful to ensure that they knew it was highly confidential. After all, I wanted to be sure that the news would reach Madrid, Dublin and London.

Chapter XXIX

MAKING A MOVE

The threat of a landing in the north seemed to have passed and our efforts were, it is fair to say, being well received throughout the rest of Ireland. The English, over the past year, had seen their influence reduced to just Dublin. The Pale had all but caved in and the influence of Essex was working for us.

I realised in retrospect that I should have gone for the jugular when I had the chance directly after the Yellow Ford. However, at the time there was a real threat that the English were to land a fleet at Lough Foyle. But now it was a different game: the English did not know what to do, the Spanish were still waiting for a sign. God alone knows how many signs the bastards needed. But we were at their whim, so we needed to play the game. So I decided to give them their sign.

We would march on the Pale. This was, I felt, next to being a useless exercise as far as progress against the English was concerned, but it might prove to be invaluable as far as maintaining support across the land was concerned. And it might at long last attract the support from Spain, which had been promised for so long.

We set out in August with just over two thousand men and made our way south through Laois and Offaly, where we were astounded by the level of support for our cause. It was truly incredible. Word of our coming had obviously preceded our arrival and we were greeted by wave after wave of jubilant locals caught up in the emotion of rebellion. After the few token raids into the Pale, where again the enthusiasm for the war was immeasurable, we made our way south into Munster. It was a truly awe-inspiring spectacle all through the country and I have never before seen such hope and happiness in the faces of the people. We were not originally going to venture as far as Munster but we were swept along by the response and I had left plenty men to defend Ulster, so we decided to press on and show our faces to our brothers in the far south. It also presented us with an ideal opportunity to call on James Fitzmaurice, the Súgan Earl, and display our support for him. At this point I would have said that the expedition had far bettered my expectations and that if you could have more than a one hundred per cent success, then a true picture would surely be closer to two hundred per cent!

There was no doubt about the unyielding support of the whole country and it seemed as though everyone was united under the Irish banner. Only a few months earlier, if I was told that the people would desert their petty differences which had held us back for so long and join as one, I would have labelled the messenger as mad. But it was true. It was happening. The Irish nation had truly been born and was already taking its first few tentative steps.

If this was not enough in the success stakes, Alonso brought word that Phillip III was raising an army for our shores and a fleet to bring it. All was well on the rebellion front and I was truly beginning to believe that victory was but a formality.

And then events took an unexpected turn.

Chapter XXX

ESSEX DECIDES

I had been informed that it was known far and wide that Essex was entering into rebellion with me and that Spain were readying another fleet for our shores. All was going well. And then I received some more news, which was quite perplexing and worrying.

'Well, Red,' I began once I had read the message, 'we have our answer: Essex has returned to England.'

'In what capacity?' asked Red.

'How do you mean?' I replied confused.

'Well, has he returned to overthrow Elizabeth? Or has he returned to repair the damage done by his enemies? Or, perhaps to press home the truce?'

'I don't know,' I replied truthfully. 'I don't think we'll ever know.'

'Stop talking in riddles, Hugh,' snapped Red, 'and tell me what the hell is going on!'

'Essex has been arrested for treason.'

'Well, if he was arrested for treason, then surely he returned on the side of our cause.'

'Not necessarily,' I replied. 'He arrived in London alone and made straight for Nonsuch, where he confronted and spoke only to Elizabeth. Nobody knows why he returned except her and my guess is that we will never know. The poor fool. He did not have many options available but why in God's holy and divine name did he choose that one? All I do know, Red, my friend, is that we will soon have yet another new Lord Deputy.'

And that new Lord Deputy, Mountjoy, was chosen but not despatched with haste, so Ormonde was again in temporary command of Elizabeth's forces. Mountjoy took over in

January 1600. I must say I'm not sure about this Mountjoy. In some ways I feel I can identify with him. Although he probably would not share that view. But I feel we have experienced similar backgrounds, just in different planes. I hail from the proudest family in all the land. The O'Neills once sat on the throne at Tara as Ard Rí (High Kings) of all Ireland. Mountjoy, Charles of the family Blount, comes from a family as old as the hills themselves. A family steeped in tradition: aristocratic, wealthy and glamorous. However, Charles' father managed to change all that. He squandered the wealth of generations in pursuit of the alchemists' philosopher's stone. My family, in comparison, managed to lose – let's qualify this – my family practically made a gift of the throne to the Normans.

Hence we both feel we have a point to prove and something to reclaim. We have both, galling as it may seem, been forced to prove our worth as a result of our upbringing and our forefathers' failings. We are both resilient, single-minded, ruthless and determined. And we both want to put an end to each other's progress.

Because of this turn of events, I decided to head north to Fortress Ulster once more and let the new Lord Deputy make the first move. Unfortunately, things did not go entirely according to plan on our march home. We knew there would be the prospect of fighting off hostile dissidents, but they would be insignificant and we would swat them like flies. However, one of the flies managed to bite back and we suffered a setback, which was immeasurable. My son-in-law and dear friend Hugh Maguire was killed in a minor skirmish and, in Hugh, I lost one of my most able leaders. There was no need for him to get that closely involved but his head was overruled by his heart and his passion for a fight ultimately cost him his life. He was a great loss for us from a military perspective, but much more than that, he was a huge loss as a friend. To this day I miss him.

Chapter XXXI

MOUNTJOY – 1600

I admire Mountjoy a great deal. Yet I know not what to make of him. Of all the English leaders sent to tackle me and the so-called Irish problem, I fear him the most. He has managed to restore a reasonable level of order to the Pale and he has all but quenched the flame of rebellion in Munster. Many have been convinced to come in and repent by Mountjoy with several lavish promises, while those who stand fast suffer the consequences. His scorched earth policy has made existence unbearable all through the country as he turns the screw. Even in Fortress Ulster, we feel the noose tighten. He has not yet managed to penetrate our defences but we are certainly restricted to our homesteads. He seems to have put great faith in learning from his predecessors' mistakes as well as imposing his own originality in style and ideas. I feel that he thinks things through a great deal and, for once, we have an English leader who respects us and our achievements. He has been careful to avoid direct conflict with us so far, and instead, he makes life exceedingly uncomfortable and erodes our influence. I never wanted that to happen. It was the last thing I expected – an English leader who respects us. The one thing I always thought I could rely on in an English commander was pure, unadulterated arrogance and a dismissive, sneering opinion towards us. This one is different. Essex labelled him as too bookish and I think he was correct. Mountjoy is certainly too bookish for my liking. He reads and learns. Essex, to his detriment, did not even read. 'Why would I need to read when my position dictates I should lead?' he was once heard to say. Well, as his reading capability is soon to be permanently removed from his shoulders, he will never learn why Mountjoy presents a far greater problem to us than he ever did himself. I feel a fitting epitaph would be 'He who rushes in head first, loses it.'

When his record is examined, Mountjoy has not achieved so much. But I feel much of that is to do with the mountain he must climb because of the stigma attached to the Blount name. Also, because of this he is constantly forced to confront the legacy of his family's enemies at Court. Her Majesty's advisors whisper incessantly in her ear terms such as 'bookish' as Essex did. But, amazingly, he still won through and received his post in Ireland. Maybe his enemies had a rethink and advised Her Misery to send him to Ireland so he should fail. In any case, I'm sure he felt that it was not the most glamorous of commissions, but certainly a challenge – a challenge he accepted gratefully. I feel Elizabeth must have a soft spot for the soft boy. There is more to him than his history suggests. There is certainly more to him than meets the eye, I am sure of it. Only time will tell how much more. Once again I am relying on my greatest ally and truest friend, Time. I just hope that my reliance is not bearing too much.

Chapter XXXII
MOUNTJOY MOVES

Much to my chagrin, Mountjoy has proved me right. He is indeed a clever and cagey customer. He obstinately refuses to attack me, so we gain no victories and the men grow restless. He does not give in to the constant whining of the babies on the council in Dublin and ignores their protests. So what does he do? He devotes his attention to ensuring we are penned in, in Ulster. We are prisoners in our own lands. All the while he puts down revolt in the remainder of the country with a great gusto, unlike Essex before him. He is in total control of his forces, which is a huge achievement considering the scum at his disposal. He forever squeezes and tightens the noose. And yet he squeezes even more.

The man has taken an ambitious gamble. His actions send a chill down my spine. He has done something I have long feared might be attempted before but not since Elizabeth has proved herself to be such a miser. But Mountjoy has obviously convinced her to go for it. I was truly shocked when I received the news.

'There must be some mistake,' I said out loud but more to myself than to the messenger.

'My Lord?' he responded, thinking I had addressed him.

'Never mind,' I said.

'Yes, my Lord,' he replied and stood awaiting a response to deliver to Red.

'Get some rest,' I said noting his eagerness. 'I need to think before I return a reply.'

'Yes, my Lord,' he replied and walked away.

This message cannot be accurate, I thought to myself. But I would swear to any number of gods that it was written by Red's own hand. So why did it read that the English had landed and established a fort at Derry and were on their way to build another further up the coast? And why did it also suggest that there were few casualties on either side and that Red was going to allow time to work in his favour?

I prepared a reply in my mind there and then and went about devising a defensive plan for the Blackwater Fort, so I could follow the messenger with haste.

When I arrived at Derry it was to find that Red's message was entirely accurate and so I attacked him for his stupidity.

'You always allow time to be the master, Hugh,' protested Red. 'What is so different on this occasion?'

'Everything!' I barked.

'Everything?' snarled Red. 'You mean you didn't think of it, so it must be wrong! Well, I'm sorry I stole your shagging thunder, Hugh, but you're not the only one around here with a brain in his head.'

'Sometimes I feel as though I am!' I snapped back.

'Watch your tongue, O'Neill,' he warned with that glint in his eye.

We stood staring at each other for a few moments, neither backing down but both attempting to cool before we said or did something we might regret.

'Look, Hugh,' began Red, 'let the stupid bastards waste their time, money and efforts on building forts. They have three and a half thousand men up here who will not venture out of their walls. We have nothing to fear. Very soon time will begin to take its toll. Hunger and disease will half their number before we know it and then we can gratefully take the forts they have kindly built for us. It will go the same as it always does at the Blackwater, Enniskillen and Ballyshannon.'

'I would love nothing more than to be proved wrong here, Red. But I feel this time is different. This Mountjoy is a different kettle of fish to his predecessors. He is a thinker, and the last thing we need is for their leader to think things through properly and devise proper plans. I would agree with you wholeheartedly if we were facing one of the previous gobshites, but we're not. We are facing a man who I feel is a brilliant soldier and who has a point to prove. He will not allow his forts to fall to rack and ruin and he will revictual them properly. Also it serves as a mental blow. They have gained a foothold in Fortress Ulster and are now forcing us to face two fronts. More than that, if Mountjoy manages to continue his line, we will be surrounded in no time. I also fear we are not yet united enough to deal with this situation.'

'That's shite, Hugh!' barked Red. 'We have never been more united than we are now. The people of Ireland would follow you to hell and back if you asked them.'

'They may have to, Red. And I am not convinced they will all come willingly. You are right when you say that we have never been more united. But it's still a fragile unity. You only have to look at Niall Garbh and Tirleach's son Arthur. Even though they fight on our side, they feel wronged. They are fairly fresh wounds that are healing, but they certainly need more time. Pressure like this might force the wounds open and add salt. We need to be extremely careful.'

'I suppose you're right there,' conceded Red. 'But you don't think after all we have been through together and all we have achieved, that they would turn their backs on us now and sell us out to the English, do you?'

'Anything is possible,' I replied. 'I trust you, Tyrrell, O'Hagan, O'Kane and a handful of others implicitly. But there are a great many others I doubt. I pray to God they prove me wrong.'

Chapter XXXIII
INVASION – 1601

The pressure was really beginning to show. Throughout 1600 and into 1601, Mountjoy had established a small chain of forts on the north coast. To all intents and purposes, they were rather ineffective, but they were certainly a boil on my arse. This was without doubt the most difficult period we had had to face in the whole of our campaign. I'm sure that some of the men were very weary and were doubting the future.

However, just when we needed a boost we got one – from Spain. It was not the ideal solution but it was certainly better than our present predicament.

'Kinsale?' bellowed Red. 'What in the name of all that is good and holy are they doing landing in fucking Kinsale? They could not have got it more wrong!'

'I don't know, my Lord,' replied the messenger practically cowering away from the raging Red and turning very pale indeed. 'That is the message I was given and I rode here in great haste, my Lord.'

'Well, did you not think to ask them why they chose to land at the wrong end of the shagging country?'

'No, my Lord. I never met them, my Lord. The message was given to me by a boy of the Earl of Desmond, my Lord.'

At this point Red turned to face me. 'How do we know this is a genuine message?' he asked.

'He had the—' began the boy.

'I was not talking to you!' barked Red without diverting his gaze from my eyes. 'Hugh, what do you make of it?'

'I think,' I said, 'that you should stop torturing this child, Red!' I replied as I got up and walked over to the boy. 'After all, he is only doing his job. Why is it, do you think,' I said to the lad, 'that the messenger always bears the brunt of the rage?'

'Because that is also our job, my Lord,' replied the boy.

'Good answer, boy! Capital answer, indeed! What is your name?' I asked.

'Sean O'Connor, my Lord.'

'Well, Sean, you seem to be a bright lad. After all, before you were interrupted by Red here, you were about to explain why you thought the message was genuine. Do continue.'

'Well, my Lord, I believe it to be true because the messenger bore the seal of the Earl of Desmond, my Lord.'

'Can you describe the seal?'

'Yes, my Lord. It was a blue badge with three yellow castles on it, my Lord.'

'Well, that is certainly the emblem. Tell me, Sean, why do you think the Spanish landed at Kinsale?'

'I would say, my Lord, that landing in the south of the country is better for them for speed between Ireland and Spain, my Lord.'

'Another good answer, Sean. However, on this occasion I think you may have got it wrong. But at least you put some thought into it. Well done! Go and get yourself down to the kitchens and get some food, drink and rest. I will call for you when I have a reply ready.'

As he left the hall, I turned to face Red who was, if anything, seething even more than he was before.

'And what was that little charade all about?' he demanded.

'The boy is the closest witness to the event we have. I wanted to gauge his feelings about the predicament with which we are now faced.'

'That's shite, Hugh. He's hardly a reliable eyewitness.'

'Agreed. But at least he thinks. Why do you think they landed at Kinsale, Red?'

'I'm not sure,' replied Red shrugging his shoulders. 'It could be that they set sail before they received news of the current state of affairs in Munster. But it could be anything. It could be that Don Juan Del Aquila doesn't know his arse from his elbow and could not navigate a shit into a bedpan.'

'Aye, there are endless possibilities. But try this one for size. The Spanish know everything about the state of the country and how the tide is slowly swinging the way of the English now this clever bastard Mountjoy is on the scene. They know that we have suffered these past few months and that we are more or less hemmed in Ulster, while throughout the country support for the cause recedes. So here is what they decided to do. They send Don Juan del Aquila to Kinsale in an effort to draw attention away from Ulster and give us some breathing space. Also, landing in Munster may also reignite the flames of passion for the fight. In the meantime, other ships land in Ulster or Connaught or maybe both.' I paused for a moment to let Red chew it over.

'Think about it, Red,' I continued. 'You know Cobos almost as well as I do. Do you think he would allow del Aquila to land in Kinsale under the current circumstances? You know what he is like – never a stone unturned.'

'That's true,' said Red. 'It's certainly feasible, I suppose. And it is the kind of thing that Cobos would dream up. But is there something we're missing?'

'Like what?'

'I don't know. I've just got a peculiar feeling about this.'

'You may well be right, Red. But how do we find out one way or the other?'

'We let Mountjoy make his move, then we evaluate the situation.'

'That may well be too late. You know what a cautious fellow he is. He has not really attacked us once. He has just made life difficult and avoided defeat by avoiding engagement.'

'Yes, but that's because he's a clever bastard, Hugh. He is without a doubt the most worthy adversary we have encountered so far. Dealing with the others was like brushing off children in comparison to tackling Mountjoy. That's why I say we let him jump first.'

'But what if he doesn't jump?' I paused long enough to see that Red wasn't sure what to do then.

'And what if he does jump and steals the march on us?' I asked.

Again, Red looked blank.

'So what do we do?' he asked.

'Well, we reply to the message by telling the Spanish that we are marching to rendezvous with them at Kinsale. Then if the message is intercepted, at least we know where Mountjoy will be heading. However, what we actually do is split our forces. You take your army through Connaught and make for west Cork county. I'll wait here awhile for fresh developments. When the time comes, I'll take my army to north Cork with or without Spanish reinforcements. Make haste to Cork and try to avoid engagements with the enemy en route and once there. If the enemy has besieged Kinsale, then our superior numbers shall surround them outside Kinsale. We will starve them out again.'

Chapter XXXIV
MY RUSE

The theory I expanded to Red was all a bit of a ruse, I must confess. It was my sincerest hope that the Spanish were sending reinforcements to Ulster and Connaught and even Munster. But it was only a hope, no more. However, my real belief was that there was a communication breakdown along the line. I was quite annoyed and disturbed by this predicament. I had fought every day of this war knowing that my network of communications was exceptional. And now in possibly our most vital hour it had failed us. If, indeed, as I suspected, del Aquila had arrived with the sole Spanish expedition, then we would be forced to fight in country alien to us and the Spanish and possibly even more like home to the English. Also, as I have alluded to previously, Mountjoy was a cunning devil and I certainly did not want to be forced into engaging on his terms. This was the real reason why I waited in Ulster. I was relying on my old friend, Time, again.

I felt that if Red and myself marched south together, everyone would be itching to fight. I had to resist that as far as I possibly could. I felt that Mountjoy would want to quench the Spanish threat as soon as humanly possible, so he would race to Kinsale and muster all his army and lay siege to the town. If this happened, Red and myself could easily then lay siege to the English and starve them into submission.

So I truly felt that the longer I tarried and delayed my march south, the more we could develop our advantage.

Chapter XXXV

RED MOVES SOUTH

Obviously I wasn't with Red when he embarked on his journey to Munster. After studying the maps for some time, we decided that the best location for Red to aim for was a small village called Bandon. He gathered his army with great haste and, considering the short time available, they were ready and moving in no time at all. That was one of the great things about our development over the years: we moved so much like a team, it was almost like watching a horse in full flight. You could see every muscle and sinew moving in complete harmony with the rest of the beast. By the end of the war, I think every one of our men could have re-enacted a day in the life of his neighbour backwards and asleep, while drunk!

However, the point of this passage is to deliver the story of Red's march with his army south to Bandon. As you know, the country was beginning to quieten as far as rebellion was concerned. I suppose it was understandable considering the fact that our victory at the Yellow Ford was nearly two years old and we had recorded nothing of note since. That alone would grey some memories, but coupled with the fact that we had failed to venture beyond our safe haven of Ulster since our excursion to Desmond when Hugh Maguire was killed, must have been a bitter bile to bear, considering the rebels had come out in support of our cause. Let alone the idea that we now had, in my mind, England's most capable general leading the counter and putting the people under much duress. Much duress! Why my understatement is practically English! The man was a savage: he was cruel and callous. He and his men watched people eat grass in an attempt to stave off starvation after his strategy of laying waste the land left them helpless. He was nothing but an imperialist pig! A swine! A bastard! A whore plying his vile trade to the virgin queen. Now, there's irony!

So, 'twas no wonder the people were turning towards them. And I mean towards them and not against us. I don't believe for a minute that they ever turned against us. They just never had a choice.

As a result of this, Red had to fight off the odd attack from previously friendly sons of Connaught and Leinster as he made his way south. However, he managed to get through Leinster and most of County Tipperary before he encountered any real trouble. And then it was huge trouble.

'That son of a whore Carew,' said Red to me, 'was waiting for us at Holycross on the Suir River. If we opted to try to outflank him on the east, sure the land is full of little tributaries of the Suir and we'd get nowhere. But on the west we had the Slieve Phelim Mountains and, at this time of the year they are nothing but bog and marsh. We didn't have the time or the resources to face him in battle. He had checked us and no mistake. I decided to consult my officers.

"'Gentlemen," says I, imitating yourself, Hugh – which got a laugh I must say – "We have what my Lord O'Neill would label a dilemma. To the east, a series of rivers and streams, which would slow us to a snail's pace. To the west, boggy mountains. To the south, Lord Carew. To the north, home and forsaking the Spaniards."

"'Well," said O'Rourke, "let's fight our way through!"

"'Do you really think we would have any chance?" says I.

"'Sure, 'tis better than trying to get through on either of the other sides only to be hacked to shreds by the bastards at their leisure.

"'That's true," says I, "but I don't think we'll get through Carew. 'Tis altogether too risky. Let's wait a couple of days for news and for O'Neill."

'This brought about a much-heated debate for and against the idea of waiting, but I had made up my mind and I was not about to budge. There was no option – we had to await developments.

'Then a truly extraordinary thing happened. Father Mulligan led us in prayer in an effort to lift our spirits.

"'Lord," he began, "give us strength in our hour of need. Show us the way. Give us a sign, oh, Heavenly Father. Lead us now as you led Moses and your chosen people out of captivity and into the promised land."

'At the time I remember thinking to myself that all was lost. The men had been low in spirits for days as we lay stranded almost in no-man's land. I even seriously contemplated retreating to Ulster and trying to meet up with yourself, Hugh, so that we could try to take Carew together. However, I decided against that course of action because we just did not have the time. So I decided to wait. It was strange but Father Mulligan's prayer seemed to have a tremendous effect. It gave the men hope and lifted their souls no end. I even found myself thinking that the priest was surely in God's good books and that we would get our sign. And we did. I swear to you that priest is blessed. Within the hour it had started to turn bitter cold. You could almost hear the ice form in the puddles. I sent a patrol to test the ground and sure enough they reported that it was firming up nicely. The Lord had given us his sign. The bitter cold and sharp frost enabled us to make the pass over the mountains and into County Limerick. I have never been more proud of my men, Hugh. They never once questioned our actions. They moved like a deer: swift and silent. We covered that march across the mountains in a single night.

'And the men went on to better that achievement. There was a grim determination buzzing through the army. You could not call it a march, but more of a sprint. Once we had conquered the mountains, we galloped south to the Bandon within a couple of days.

'That bastard Carew gave good chase almost all the way. He must have realised the significance of that frost as much as we did and so my cautious approach paid off. "Red Hugh O'Donnell playing a cautious card?" I hear you ask. But it is indeed true. I tell you, Hugh, you would have been proud of me. I thought that Carew would be too clever to miss the opportunity the frost presented to us that night and I was right. We must have broke camp at more or less the same time. And I was proved right to drive beyond Cashel. For my scouts in the rear informed me later that Cashel was where Carew came in to intercept us. As I said before, he chased us hard. But we moved faster and he gave up eventually and took the crow's flight to Kinsale to join Mountjoy. I tell you, man, by the time we reached the Bandon, we were glad of the rest. And we had earned it.'

Chapter XXXVI

THE PRESSURE MOUNTS

I followed Red shortly after his miraculous escape, although I took my route through the midlands, as the way was now open for me. As I said before, I sent Red on ahead of me deliberately, so I could delay any potential action until I was completely ready. But I could not put off my move indefinitely and it was with a heavy heart that I left my Catherine.

'Why don't you let me join you?' she asked as the pain of parting I felt in my heart told all too plainly on my face.

'We have been through this, my love,' I said with a sigh. 'It will be dangerous. You would hate every waking minute of it, and besides, I will not be away that long – two months at the very most.'

'I don't care,' she replied. 'I don't want us to be apart for two minutes let alone two months.' She embraced me and started crying.

'I know,' I said. 'And you know that I feel the same way, but you also know that it is for the best that you remain here.' And with that I held her as though I would never see her again. Then I left.

We marched south immediately and made good time reaching Bandon in just ten days. As soon as I arrived the arguments began. Obviously, Red and del Aquila wanted to attack. I, on the other hand, did not. And we each argued our points vociferously.

'Well, Hugh, I have other interests which need protection,' blasted Red. 'You know as well as I do that Niall Garbh will have set about raiding my lands as soon as I moved south. So I want this thing ended as quickly as possible so I can go home.'

'Will you just listen to reason, Red?' I replied. 'Garbh will already have done his worst by now. The state your lands are in now is the same state they will be in by the time we move north again. You know this to be true. Now let's do this thing properly and protect our resources as well as we possibly can. Why should we lose men and ammunition fighting Mountjoy, when the ruthless bastard will be eating grass in his lunacy in a few short weeks?'

'We don't know that for sure!' snapped Red. 'All we have to go on is a few tall tales from your mysterious sources.'

'Red, I will not listen to this drivel. You know as well as I do that my sources have proved themselves accurate time after time. So don't dare to doubt them now. Jesus, man, you know that not a grain of corn has managed to get through to the enemy via land these past weeks and our reports suggest that the winds make it impossible for their ships to provide relief and resource. More than that, 'tis bitter cold and they face the harshest of elements out in the open in their camp. They are defeated as long as we tarry. Let's savour the moment and prolong their agony.'

'No! Hugh, you must appreciate what kind of affect a crushing victory over them would have with the Spaniards. Within weeks we would have double the men we requested and a fleet ready to take the war to England.'

'And we will achieve that crushing defeat over the English by starving them out, humiliating them and letting their cries of agony be heard around the world. No Englishman will ever want to set foot in Ireland again and the world will know that we are clever and cunning and that great English generals fall by the wayside like leaves in the autumn.'

'But think how better it would be if we destroyed them in a pitched battle. The world would surely quake knowing that the English were defeated at their own game.'

'This is lunacy, Red!' I spat. 'We will never beat the English like that. We must fight our way. They know Munster better than us – Carew has served here long enough. We don't have the comfort of our forests and mountains. You have seen the terrain. You can see for miles and that is just what Mountjoy would want. It is everything that our Fortress Ulster is not and we are not suited to it.'

'I want to fight. The men want to fight. The Spaniards want to fight. Del Aquila labels us cowards. What is wrong with you? Let's win back our honour, stand up and be counted and fight!'

'Have you run out of arguments, then?' I asked.

'What kind of a question is that?' spat Red.

'Simply that you have put forward a constructive reasoning for fighting up until your last eruption. Let del Aquila say what he likes. He is just trying to goad us into taking action, and were it up to you, he would succeed. I know the men want to fight – they are soldiers, after all. I know the Spanish want to fight for exactly the same reason and also because they feel hemmed in. And I know you want to fight because it is in your nature. I don't want to fight, Red, if we don't have to. I cannot see the point if we can achieve a bloodless victory. I'm no coward but I have had a fill of fighting and bloodshed and death these past six years and I am sick of it. I want this war to be over, but by God I want it to end with us as victors. And I believe the best way to achieve victory this day is to starve the English into submission, desperation and defeat. And that is what we are going to do.'

'We are starving ourselves, Hugh!' retorted Red. 'Christ, man, we carried our food on our backs. We get the odd gift from locals and we scrounge off the land, but we are hardly scoffing caviar and swilling champagne while the English resort to cannibalism! And you have heard from del Aquila – they feel blessed if they manage to snare a scrawny flea-bitten moggy. Between us we are no better off than the English. What makes you so sure they will succumb first?'

'Because at least we can look to the land and the people. We can also ensure that any victuals sent through for the relief of Mountjoy and Carew fall into our hands. And we can deprive the bastards of everything.'

'Ach, man, 'tis easier said than done and well you know it. 'Tis pointless trying to make you see reason anymore.' And with that Red stormed off, his blood still boiling.

Chapter XXXVII
PRINCIPLES

How blind can men be? Or am I the only one who can see that we must not attack the English under any circumstances. We have succeeded thus far in this war by employing similar tactics and have gradually progressed our situation. The result of this strategy is the arrival of the Spanish. Now we must convince them to stay. We must be clever about this. Or am I wrong? Can we really crush Mountjoy if we attack? I think not. It is obvious that most of the others do. But then again everybody thought the world was flat until Columbus proved otherwise. I'll stand by my principles and use patience and time. Mountjoy wants us to attack. My very bones tell me this, so I'll not attack.

Our position, as I have said before, has progressed gradually. Once we put paid to Mountjoy, I fully expect it to progress rapidly. But we must approach this situation in the correct manner. Then the Spanish will send more assistance and the English will be virtually non-existent in the country.

Why the hurry?

Chapter XXXVIII
CONCESSION

I believe I have made a terrible mistake, which could have disastrous consequences. I have conceded and agreed to attack the English the day after tomorrow – Christmas Eve. I felt I could hold Red and del Aquila off no longer. And I fear that our cause is now in serious peril.

It all came to a head this afternoon when Bustamente arrived with a message from del Aquila.

'My Lord O'Neill,' he greeted upon entering my quarters. 'My Lord O'Donnell,' he continued turning and bowing to Red after he had done the same to me.

'What news?' I asked.

'My Lord O'Neill, I am the bearer of grave news this day. My Lord Don Juan del Aquila says that he cannot hold the enemy off for much longer and that if we do not decide on a strategy for attack, that he will be forced to retreat from Kinsale, put to sea and return to Spain.'

'What nonsense!' I rebuked. 'The English can pound away at the walls of Kinsale until doomsday and they will not breach them.'

'I think,' began Red, 'that Del Aquila is in a far better position to assess the situation, Hugh. We cannot afford to lose him. Now let's agree to attack.'

'No!' I raged. 'How many times do I have to say that we will be playing into Mountjoy's hands if we attack. It's what he wants us to do. *I* know it. *You* know it, Red. *You* know it, senor Bustamente. And del Aquila knows it.'

'But if we don't attack, del Aquila will leave us. You just heard the same thing yourself. And then Mountjoy will have Kinsale and he will turn his attention on us!'

'My Lords,' said Bustamente, 'I believe that my Lord del

Aquila was serious about his threat to leave.'

'I don't doubt it for a moment,' I replied, 'but we must try to make him see sense. We hold all the advantages right now. We cannot afford to lose the initiative to Mountjoy. We must plead with del Aquila to wait but a few more days.'

'Do you think Lord del Aquila will listen and heed this advice?' asked Red.

'My Lord O'Donnell, I know not what my Lord del Aquila will do. But I do know that he grows more frustrated by the hour.'

'Then we must act,' said Red. 'Tell your Lord del Aquila that I will attack at an agreed hour.'

'I will, my Lord O'Donnell,' said Bustamente, and he bowed and turned to leave.

'Don't you dare tell your Lord del Aquila any such thing!' I screamed. 'Since when do you decide on our strategy before we have reached agreement?' I demanded of Red.

'Who said anything about us?' replied Red. 'I will attack and anyone else who wishes to join me is more than welcome. I will not speak for you, Hugh, but we must take action.'

'Have you lost your mind, man? This is completely insane! You know that if we attack the English with half strength, we will be destroyed. Tell me you are not serious about this half-witted scheme.'

'Oh, but I am deadly serious, Hugh,' replied Red calmly. 'We have no alternative. If we fail to act now, we may as well head home to the north and forget about the whole affair because we will lose Spain. I am attacking and that is my final decision.'

'Listen to reason, Red…' I began.

'No! We must attack. It's that simple.'

'Do not force my hand, Red. I'll not back you on some foolhardy mission just because I know you have no chance on your own.'

'Then join me in the attack because together and with the Spaniards we can and we will win.'

'I wish I shared your faith,' I said and sighed. 'I have been left with no alternative,' I said with resignation. 'Let's decide on a time.'

Chapter XXXIX
CARPE DIEM

Perhaps Red, del Aquila and all the others are right and we should be able to defeat Mountjoy. What am I talking about? Of course, they are right! Mountjoy is surrounded and in receipt of no supplies. His men are hungry, sick and weak. His forces dwindle by the day as disease and desertion ravage his ranks. We outnumber them on our own, and with the Spaniards on our side; I would estimate that we have at least a two to one advantage in strength. Why should I worry? If we remain disciplined and controlled, we will secure an easy victory. And then we can strengthen our defences throughout the whole of Ireland with the help of the Spaniards. Philip III will no doubt send a bigger fleet immediately to ensure we secure the entire country and then he will send regular convoys of supplies and men. We have nothing to fear and everything to gain.

I think I must be so used to conducting our defence using the same old tactics that I have become set in my ways. These tactics are no longer necessary, I am sure of it. And so I will bid a fond farewell to my mistress, Time, for I have a new love – Speed.

It is time to seize the moment.

Chapter XL
KINSALE

Christmas Eve, 3 a.m. Time to move. So I gave the order and slowly we began our march. The fact that the element of surprise was essential to our success meant that not a word was spoken, not a match was struck and not a sound was heard. We felt our way in the darkness and the silence and there was an eerie, almost deathly atmosphere, which accompanied our every step. I could feel that the men were nervous. We had never fought a battle at night before and nobody really knew what to expect. What we had imagined and prepared the men for was to find the enemy asleep, hungry and in no order for fighting. However, we stressed that this may not be the case and so we left one final ambiguous instruction – be prepared for anything. It's a strange thing but in any given situation we tend to play out different scenarios in our minds, which help us to prepare for what lies ahead. So issuing a contingency instruction like 'Be prepared for anything' is next to useless. So, as we moved towards our quarry, I could sense that not a soul really knew what was going to happen and that all kinds of horrors were being played out in thousands of minds.

It was a painstakingly slow march because of the dark and the need for stealth. And the time only contrived to make things worse for us. Much like the waiting at Clontibret, we had too much time for thinking and that is a dangerous thing for a man going into battle.

We trudged on. And then we were there. We could see the English camp in the distance, so we halted.

Now we just had to coordinate with Red, Richard and del Aquila. But there was no sign of Red. The time for the attack was six o'clock. We just had to wait. I could smell victory and it smelled good.

Then just as I was preparing patrols, it happened.

This cannot be! I screamed inside. My face must have been the picture of pure horror momentarily. The English were ready for battle. In fact, they attacked us first! I managed to gather myself after my momentary lapse and delivered orders to the men as though this was exactly what I had been expecting. There was no sign of Red. I did not know whether Tyrrell had managed to link up with del Aquila, and we were facing the enemy alone. I drew back over a bog where we had a better chance of beating off the attack. The men were superb. The attack was repulsed, resisted and driven off. The men cheered and yelped with joy as they saw the Sassenachs flee. And then disaster struck: a second wave of their attack, far stronger than the first, came at us. It must have been three hundred strong in horse. The delight of the men ebbed away as quickly as it had flowed in and was replaced by panic. The ranks broke and the English wheeled after the weak links. It was clear that the first attack was repelled by a reactive instinct, which was instilled in the men through all their years of training. But once the first attack was repulsed and the joy of our little success subsided, the thought seemed to filter through the men that the English were not supposed to be ready for the battle. *We* were supposed to surprise them. They should have been sleeping. We did not have the element of surprise on our side. Indeed, in a cruel and ironic twist of fate, it was the English who surprised us. My few horse fled in an instant and the ranks of the infantry opened up to let them through. I and my officers immediately set about rallying the troops and solidifying our line.

We closed ranks and retreated through a small scrub I had spied, which made it impossible for the English cavalry to follow. A brief reprieve. But too many had panicked and fled from our ranks. My priority now was to get clear of the scrub, calm the men and reassure them that we could turn this around. As we cleared the scrub, we stumbled upon Red just as the English came around to attack again. Confusion reigned. The English broke through splitting the ranks again. Now the panic was ungovernable. All my calming words and reassuring tones had no effect. My authority, which had been followed unquestionably for more than a decade, was now an alien language. Were these not the same men who fought by my side at Clontibret, the Yellow

Ford and a host of others? Were these not the same stalwarts who had suffered a dozen reverses and yet kept the faith? Were these not the same soldiers who were told to always be prepared for anything? Aye, they were all of these and more besides. And yet they crumbled in an instant. Why? I'll never know. All I do know is that despite my efforts I could not allay their panic and fear and soon enough I cut a desperate and forlorn figure drowning in my misfortune. I was clutching at straws in a vain effort to regain control. I was in a surreal land of nightmares.

Keep the men together, I said to myself. God blast it, where is del Aquila? Stand your ground. Stand your ground! Fight, fight! Don't run!

But the men were panicking. No need to panic, I screamed inside. The Spaniards will be here soon. Where was del Aquila? Where were the Spaniards? They should be attacking. I felt numb. I felt ashamed, embarrassed, humiliated. Where were the Spaniards? Stand and fight. We can turn this around. Stand and fight. Guns booming. Horses galloping. Men screaming. Men whooping. Swords clashing. Here come the English again on horseback. Cutting, hacking, slashing, stabbing, beating, hacking, hacking, hacking, killing, slaughtering, butchering. And we are running. Stop running. Stand and fight.

And then I lost it and started screaming at them. 'Stop running! Turn and face the enemy! Turn and fight! We stand a better chance if we turn and fight! That's an order, God damn you! Obey me! Stand and fight, stand and fight, stand and fight! Stand and fight…'

Where in heaven and hell was del Aquila? Why were the Spaniards not attacking? Where was del Aquila? Where was del Aquila? How did Mountjoy know? I smell a rat. I am caught like a rat. Rats deserting the sinking ship. Rats, rats, rats. We are all rats. We are lost. All is lost. We are defeated.

No option but to retreat. 'Retreat! Retreat!'

We keep on running. Still they chase us. Hacking, cutting, slashing, butchering, slashing, jeering, cheering, shouting, whooping.

Tired, exhausted, drained, shattered, disillusioned, defeated, destroyed. Don't care anymore. Let the bastards suffer their fate.

They deserve it. Just want to die. Take me now, God, you vindictive bastard!

They have given up the chase. They are too tired and weak from the hunger. For that we are grateful. An hour. The whole thing took only an hour. Not our finest hour. Our most significant, yes, but not our finest.

Chapter XLI
THE HORROR

The enemy cut and slashed and hacked away at the men as they ran from the battle. The fear and panic washed over us like a huge wave and swept the men away with it. Could they not see that they stood a better chance of survival if they turned and fought and stood united? Could they not see that it was pointless running from men on horseback? No, evidently not. They panicked and fled. It was absolutely heartbreaking. This was exactly the kind of battle the Sassenachs enjoyed. Their whoops of delight could be heard for miles around. Yes, they enjoyed a fight that wasn't a fight – a fight against a disorganised and practically defenceless running rabble. This was never a battle. This was a slaughter. As I had predicted after our victory at the Biscuits, they pursued their advantage as far as they could.

We lost more men that day than we had during the entire preceding seven years of war. It was a disaster, a fiasco greater than we could ever have imagined.

Chapter XLII

THE DEMON BOTTLE

The sense of doom which now hung over the men was unbelievable. Sure, it was a defeat but we had suffered a couple of reverses previously in the war – albeit Kinsale was the heaviest defeat we had endured. But it was not the defeat alone, which filled the air with doom.

For so long I had spoken of Spanish aid. And when it eventually arrived, our confidence soared. All of a sudden our dream became a reality and I think the men truly believed for the first time that we would drive the English from Ireland forever. I'm convinced that there were many who found it difficult to believe how much we had achieved on our own. There were more still who had grown so much in stature, confidence and belief that we didn't need the Spanish and that eventually we would sap the English into submission. So when the Spaniards did arrive, it was almost taken for granted that victory would soon follow.

However, the shocking defeat at Kinsale stunned everyone. Not just Red and myself. Not only Richard and all my officers and men. But the English, the Spanish, His Holiness, the Pope and all who took an interest in the proceedings were also dumbfounded by it.

All that confidence and self-belief that had been built up in nearly ten long years vanished in that hour. But more than the despair and disbelief – which hung in the air like the stench of the dead on a battlefield, another emotion came to the fore and dominated our hearts – shame. We were ashamed of ourselves. All of our training and tactics, all we had learned in the past decade, all our plans, all our discipline and patience deserted us in our hour of need. It just evaporated into the air. The men as one were consumed by a cowardly demon, which turned the clock back and transformed them into a rowdy, ill-disciplined, barbarous rabble once more. And the shame that we allowed this to happen hung over us. I tell you now that on that morning I wept. And I wasn't alone. Many of the men shed silent tears as we trudged mournfully in our forced retreat.

As I said before, we had suffered defeats previously in our struggle, but when we were beaten we could always hold our head high and know that we fought bravely and did all we could. Alas, on this occasion, we could not.

We trudged on until we reached Innishannon and there I decided to halt and assess the situation. I called my officers together for a council.

'Well,' I began, 'can anyone explain that debacle this morning?'

Silence hovered in the air above heads hung low.

'My men are tired, hungry, cold and sick of war, Hugh,' said Burke. 'They want to go home.'

'We are all in the same boat,' I replied. 'But that is not a reason to give up. And I'm sure you don't believe it to be a valid reason either. You're just trying to change a delicate subject. Now, I'll ask again, what went wrong?'

'Hugh,' said Red, 'let's put this morning out of our heads and focus on the future.'

'And learn nothing?' I bellowed. 'What kind of a shagging future do you think that will bring us, Red?'

'Don't dare to talk to me like that, Hugh. It wasn't my fault!' he replied.

'No? Then who is to blame, Red? I'll tell you who, me. It's my fault. And all of you. And del Aquila. And all of the men – dead and alive. And I don't care if that sounds disrespectful. The cowardly fools ran and were butchered as a result. We are all at fault and there is no easy way to repair the damage. I doubt that we will ever receive any help from Spain again.'

'Let's go back to Kinsale and reverse the situation,' suggested Red.

A general uproar greeted this remark, which told its own tale. Nobody was willing to return to Kinsale.

'Gentlemen! Gentlemen!' I shouted. 'Let's return to calm!'

Order returned and all ears focused once more.

'It's this simple,' I began. 'We witnessed today what we all feared deep down: that while we have made significant progress with training the men to act with discipline, there is still much work to do. The old problems appeared this morning like they had never been away. And that, gentlemen, is why we failed.'

'It's not the only thing, Hugh,' said O'Rourke. 'What about the Spanish? Where were they?'

'I don't know,' I replied simply.

'And you, Red,' said Art, 'how come you were so late?'

'We got lost,' replied Red with an embarrassed shrug of his shoulders. 'It's alien country to us and we lost our way in the dark.'

It was a savage irony that Red managed to drive his men across the Slieve Phelim Mountains into Limerick and on to the Bandon in the pitch of night without a hitch – a march of some fifty-odd miles. Yet a three-mile fumble in the dark managed to foil him.

'What I want to know is how were the English ready for us?' asked Red. 'The element of surprise was to be our greatest weapon. How did we manage to forfeit it?'

'Maybe the messenger never got through to del Aquila and it was intercepted by the English instead,' said Art.

'No,' I replied. 'I spoke to Bustamente on his return and he assured me that he got through.'

Nobody questioned this as nobody doubted del Aquila's messenger Bustamente who had made the trip from del Aquila to ourselves tirelessly over and over again for the past few days and had shown remarkable courage without a grumble.

The ideas then dried up and everyone remained silent in thought until it was broken by MacMahon's messenger rushing in. It was only then that I really noticed MacMahon's absence from the meeting.

'My Lords,' said the boy bowing.

'You have a message from your master?' I asked.

'No, my Lord,' he replied.

'Then what brings you here, lad? Why do you interrupt our meeting?'

'My Lord, I have left my master. He betrayed us.'

This news gave rise to a cacophonous commotion as men leapt

to their feet and made to get at the boy and rip out his insolent tongue. He was protected by Red with his sword drawn who demanded that the would-be assailants desist and hear what the boy had to say.

'Go on,' he said to the lad when it had settled down again.

'My Lords, the night before last my master sent me to the camp of Captain William Taafe to ask his old friend for a bottle of whiskey as my master's rack had run dry. Captain Taafe duly obliged and I raced back with due haste to present my master with his *uisce beatha*...'

'That doesn't make MacMahon a traitor,' bellowed O'Rourke.

'Let the boy finish, O'Rourke,' said I. 'Continue, lad.'

'Then yesterday my master sent me with a letter to Captain Taafe once more. I cannot read or write, so I knew not its content. I thought he might be requesting more whiskey as he had finished the other bottle in but a few short hours. However, Captain Taafe read the letter and smiled broadly. He was as excited as a wee puppy about to be fed from his master's table. He then called in one of his officers and ordered him to get a messenger ready as he had received wonderful news and he must inform his Lord Mountjoy at once. He said that the rebels would attack this night and that they must make ready for battle. When I heard this, I was taken with a great horror and I dashed for the entrance of his tent. I was too quick for both Captain Taafe and his lieutenant but they came rushing out after me and ordered that I must be captured. I was then swarmed by all the men standing by. I couldn't escape, much as I tried. I wanted to get to you, my Lords, so I could warn you, but I failed.' At this the boy broke down and wept.

I scanned the room and have never seen so many solemn, sombre and despairing faces in my life. Nobody doubted his tale of woe. I returned my gaze to the boy.

'Then what happened, lad?' I asked.

'They held me until after the battle, my Lord. When the fighting was over, their men returned rejoicing and I knew we were defeated. They let me go a short while later as I could do no more harm to their efforts this day.'

'Well,' I said, 'the puzzle is complete, gentlemen. All we tried to eradicate from our soldiers, indeed, from our way of life returns to haunt us. We even have the token, cowardly traitor who could not miss the sup for a solitary day.'

'I'll castrate the bastard if ever I get my hands on him,' said Burke.

'And what will that prove?' asked Tyrrell.

'It will make an example of the swine for all other potential traitors,' replied Burke.

'It will make you feel less of a woman after running away screaming this morning,' countered Tyrrell.

'You'll pay for that, you English scum!' raged Burke drawing his sword.

Red got between them and held Burke's sword arm firm. Others rushed to assist Red. Tyrrell merely stood his ground, eyeing Burke coldly. Eventually, Burke stopped struggling to get free and allowed his sword to be taken.

'Pistols at dawn, then,' he spat and threw his gauntlet into Tyrrell's face.

'Putting a bullet through your spineless heart will afford me great pleasure,' retorted Tyrrell.

'Oh, for the sake of all that is holy,' I said, 'have we not had enough disasters for one day? There will be no duelling or fighting amongst ourselves. Since we left the north, we seem to have forgotten how to think. It's almost like we left our brains up there after us. Now we have far more important matters to discuss than resolving petty differences. I want to know what we're going to do. I believe we should return to Kinsale and finish the job the right way. Let's starve them into submission. Del Aquila suggested that they were tired, hungry and demoralised, in any case. Now they will certainly have gained a boost by their victory today, but how much of that morale will be sapped by the sight of us returning? I put it to you that it is the only course of action we can take.'

The only sound was the shuffling of feet and some nervous coughing.

'Does nobody want revenge?' I ventured.

'Our men will not return, Hugh,' said O'Rourke. 'If we return to Kinsale, it will be with less than half our strength.'

'So do you think we should go home to the north and sit out

the winter and resume the struggle come the spring?'

This had a few takers but I think the truth of the matter was that they did not know what they should do.

'I say we get some revenge in a different fashion,' said O'Rourke. 'We'll make for Dublin and the Pale. It is practically unguarded at the moment. It's an easy target and it will be a huge humiliation for Mountjoy.'

This suggestion seemed to raise spirits no end as many voices shared O'Rourke's enthusiasm for his scheme.

I, however, did not. 'Are you incapable of learning? Is listening beyond you?' I spurted. 'Mountjoy does not care one jot for the snotty-nosed spoilt children of the Pale. He would sooner do away with the lot of them in any case. The last thing he will do is rush to their assistance while del Aquila sits in Kinsale with our Spanish hopes.'

'Exactly,' spurted O'Rourke beaming like he had just solved the mystery to end all mysteries. 'If Mountjoy refuses to defend them, then we can do what we wish.'

'In the name of God, man,' blasted Red, 'are you no better than a feckin' Viking? Raiding, pillaging, plundering, raping, beating defenceless, weak opposition? Is that the extent of your abilities and aims? Hugh knows that to win this war we must face the English. Had you not gathered that much? If we are to drive them out, we must defeat them and make it impossible for them to return. We cannot afford to desert the Spaniards because we need their help. We cannot win this war without them, and if we desert them, they will not assist us again. We must return to Kinsale – there is no other option. And this time I'm with Hugh. This time we besiege the bastards and starve them into submission.'

'I'm not going back, Red,' raged O'Rourke. 'My men would slit my throat if I even suggested it.'

'I'm with O'Rourke,' said Burke. 'It's sheer madness to return.'

'And I,' the chorus rang out with the majority.

'Don't you see that we have no choice?' said Red almost begging. 'We must keep Spain with us.'

'We were doing fine without them,' countered Burke. 'It's all gone against us since they finally fulfilled the promise of so long. They land at the wrong end of the shagging country and force us to march hundreds of miles to assist them while our lands are left defenceless behind us! I thought they were supposed to be assisting us! And then at the appointed hour they don't even make an appearance. Was it too cold for the black fuckers to get out of their nice warm beds in the nice cosy cottages of Kinsale while we slept drenched in freezing cold ditches? In my mind, they are a bunch of useless, queer cowards and we are better off without them. I say we head home, defend our lands this winter and resume our struggle come the spring. 'Tis better to live now and run away, for we'll live to fight another day.'

The cacophony that greeted this little speech was deafening, and I must say that on the surface Burke had made a fine point. The arrival of the Spanish had been a disaster from start to finish.

'Well, gentlemen,' I began rising to my feet and restoring some order, 'if you refuse to return to Kinsale, I feel we have no option but to beat a speedy retreat home to the north.' I could have argued about Spain's value to us but what was the point? I had made the same argument one hundred times before.

This was greeted with a chorus of cheers but I was far from cheery. Everything that Red had said was true. We needed the Spaniards. And there was no way they would return if we deserted them now. Through my previous efforts I knew his Holiness the Pope would not get involved in a war. If only it were one of his more volatile predecessors – some of them really enjoyed a good war, the murdering, corrupt bastards! I also felt that King James VI of Scotland was against the idea of war with England. I didn't know where else to turn.

At that moment I felt completely defeated. However, we could not surrender. Not now. Not here. We had to get home and assess the situation there.

'Well, I'm not returning home!' bellowed Red, startling me from my thoughts.

'What?' said O'Rourke. 'You can't fight the English alone, Red! And your men, no matter how loyal they are, will not follow you into certain death. Don't be a fool, Red. Come home.'

'No,' answered Red. 'I'm not going north. But I'm not going

back to Kinsale either. I'm going to Spain. Alone. I'm going to get an audience with King Phillip III and I'm going to convince him to send the help we need.'

'Good man!' said Burke. 'That will give the men the hope they need to carry on.'

'Rory,' said Red to his brother, 'you are the O'Donnell by proxy until I return.'

I could not believe that our predicament was getting worse by the minute. I would need Red once we returned north to help me keep the men united. He would not succeed in Spain, I was certain of it. I shrugged and sighed and listened to my world collapsing.

Chapter XLIII
THE WORMS TURN –1602

I feel I have gained a fairly accurate insight into the feelings of Our Lord when the Jews demanded freedom for Barrabas and crucifixion for Himself. The people have turned and betrayed us. The very souls we fought for and gave hope to have joined ranks with our enemy. Only a few months ago were these men and women coming out in rebellion with us and swelling our numbers united in one Irish cause. They fought with us side by side in our attempt to rid the land of the English blight. And now they pledge allegiance to the royal slut. It is more galling than anyone can imagine. I cannot explain my feelings right now, but suffice it to say that I am certainly more bitter towards my turncoat countrymen than ever I was towards the English. Why did I even bother? I gave up everything for the ungrateful bastards and this is how they repay me. Not just me either: Red, Art, Cormac, Maguire. Maguire even lost his life for them. Tyrrell, I mean for God's sake, Tyrrell is English! An Englishman gave up more for their freedom than they did themselves. And Tyrrell is not the only Englishman who threw in his lot with us. It sickens me. It brings shame on our nation.

Chapter XLIV
SIX DAYS

I have received news from a friend in Dublin this day. Actually it can hardly be called news as it is over a week old. He wrote on the night before we attacked the English. His messenger could not read, and in any case, the seal remained intact and so the boy could not know its content or he would not have bothered to complete his task. The information is now useless but how valuable it could have been. My friend was reliably informed that the day before we attacked, the English troops' rations were reduced to a quarter of the standard daily allowance. Even at this miserable rate their supplies would have lasted but six days. Six days! Six godforsaken, miserable, shagging days. If only I had received this information before the attack. *If* only Red and del Aquila had listened. *If* only I was stronger. *If* only. *If* is without a doubt the biggest word in the language and the one I hate the most.

Chapter XLV
RETREAT AND REVENGE

The relentless attacks from the traitors keep coming even as we near our home of Ulster. These locusts from Munster, Leinster and Connaught have plagued us incessantly on our long retreat home. Not only are we being forced to swat these bloodsucking insects as we go, but we are fending off a strong English Army with the taste of victory on their tongues. Once we reach Ulster we can regroup, dig in and wait for Red and the Spanish. We will launch our counter-offensive in the spring and when Mountjoy has been driven off, we will take sweet vengeance on the traitorous scum who do not deserve to call themselves Irish.

Chapter XLVI
BLAME

I suppose, when I think about it sometimes, I can't blame the people for deserting me. At the end of the day it matters not whether they pay taxes to and serve an English Queen, a Spanish King or an Irish Rí. It is still some high and mighty aristocratic buffoon who makes their lives that little more difficult. Why should they care that the buffoon should be me?

Even if they did believe that I could be of benefit to them, in their eyes I have failed them. Actually, not just in their eyes but also, in the eyes of the world. All I have brought to these people is nearly a decade of war, death and destruction. And now as Mountjoy persecutes me across the country like a rabid dog, I have brought them the very real prospect of famine.

No, I can't help feeling bitter about them turning against me, but I also cannot blame them for feeling betrayed.

Chapter XLVII
PERSECUTION

Is nobody with us? Even in Ulster the people have turned. We are forced to find shelter and food in the mountains and forests. And yet the English drive on. Surely they must be as weary as we are. We are drained to nothing. We are forced to forage for food and find barely enough to keep us alive. Just enough for a heartbeat. We cannot go on like this for much longer. Morale has ebbed away and none of the men hold out much hope anymore. I am sure they feel we are defeated. The only reason they do not desert me is because they have nowhere else to go. If only Red would land with the Spaniards. It would raise our spirits no end. Damn Mountjoy! Does the man never rest?

Chapter XLVIII
HOPE AND DREAMS

It seems that nothing goes for us. Not only have the people turned against us, but also the cold cripples us, illness ravages our numbers and food is becoming an increasingly scarce commodity. The icy hand of death hovers over our every step. And the English seem to grow ever more determined.

In my dreams I find comfort and warmth in my castle at Dungannon. But when I awake I am faced with the grim relentlessness of reality. At times I come close to giving up but I must put my men first. I am sure they feel the same but I wonder if they realise what may happen should we surrender.

Surely we must hear from Red soon.

Chapter XLIX
RED

I eventually received news of Red today. *He's dead.*

Red was only in Spain for five weeks. He had two appointments with King Phillip III, which were proving fruitful. His dynamism and enthusiasm infected the King as it had done so many others. He had convinced him to support our cause and Phillip promised immediate assistance and was busy raising an army and a fleet at Cadiz. Rumour has it that an assassin followed Red to Spain and, when he got his chance, poisoned him. Red died two weeks later after an agonising, excruciating battle as the poison ravaged his innards.

In many ways I feel that our last spark of enthusiasm died with Red. No man was ever born who was better at rallying people to a cause than Red. I will miss him.

Chapter L
NO OPTION

It's over. Our last hope is gone. Red's expedition to Spain was truly the only cast of the die left for us and it is gone. After I heard of his death, I waited a few days to think things over and try to come up with another plan. However, I truly believe that we are beaten. I will send a message to Mountjoy asking for a parley which I am convinced he will grant. He is a gentleman and I'm sure he will want an honourable end to this tragedy. But first I must consult my kinsmen.

I'm weary. We are all weary. This war has gone on for far too long and everybody is sick of it. Now it needs to end.

'I have some news to impart,' I began, 'which will put our predicament into stark perspective for you. I am afraid that Red Hugh O'Donnell, Earl of Tir Connell, is dead. He was poisoned by an English spy as he courted King Phillip III of Spain. There will not be a second fleet from Spain and we are now alone.'

I allowed this news to sink in for a moment before continuing.

'I now feel,' I said, 'that our position is untenable. We have no hope of securing victory and I believe surrender is our only option. However, I will not take any action until you have all had your say but I urge you to join me and end it now. I think we should make a decision as soon as possible, so I would suggest that we meet and decide at noon tomorrow.'

'Why wait until tomorrow when we know today?' said Art. 'We are beaten and we cannot go on. I say we surrender now.'

'No!' bellowed O'Kane, 'I say we give it a few days. The Spaniards may have decided to set sail even though Red is dead. And besides, how do we know for sure that Red died over there? That message could just be a trap set by the English. They are certainly cunning and unscrupulous enough for a trick like that.'

184

'That is certainly true,' said Cormac. 'Let's wait for now. We have seen off the worst of the cold weather. Spring is nearly here and the English have been unable to find us these past few months. Let's give it a short while and wait for news from Spain.'

'Stop talking nonsense!' wailed Art. 'There is no hope left and we are beaten. That is how simple it is.'

'We don't know that for certain,' said Cormac. 'What harm will a few more days do?'

Art threw his eyes heavenward in despair.

'We will wait,' I said. 'We will ensure that we receive official news from Spain. We will not submit only to discover that we were tricked by the English.'

Art bit his tongue, but we all knew in our hearts that he was right.

Chapter LI

TULLAHOGUE

That bastard, Mountjoy, makes my life a living hell on this godforsaken Earth. He demolishes my life around me and delights in torturing my soul. He scored another victory of the mind some days ago when his men reached Dungannon. They took the castle with little resistance and proceeded on to Tullahogue. This, as you know, is the seat of O'Neill power and has been for centuries. Generations of the clan have flocked to Tullahogue to witness the inauguration of the new O'Neill at the death or resignation of the old Rí.

Mountjoy's men destroyed this sacred spot and burned it down to a scrubby, barren patch. However, this was not done until he had first smashed the ancient stone throne to pieces. On this throne *the* O'Neill was handed the reigns of power since time immemorial and now it would never happen again. If ever he wanted to send a message that the game was up, then this was it. Step by step he is raping my ancient culture and erasing the clan from existence. The net is closing. There is no hope of escape. I must do the only thing in my power and surrender.

Chapter LII
SURRENDER – 1603

And so I came in and surrendered. I did what I had to and I submitted on my knees to Mountjoy. We then travelled to Dublin where I was forced to re-enact the whole charade once more for the cowardly, snivelling council's benefit. It was bad enough having to submit to an adversary as worthy as Mountjoy, but to have to swear to that pack of sewer rats was intolerable. And then the third and final time would be to the Queen herself once we moved onto England and London.

However, after my submission in Dublin, we received some news, which would affect proceedings. Elizabeth was dead. In fact, she had been dead for some days since. She was dead before I surrendered. Mountjoy and the council had known this but had forced me to swear allegiance to a dead monarch. This meant that the whole thing was null and void, but I was caught and could not escape. When I heard the news of her death, the enormity of it hit me immediately. Had I but stayed in the field a day or two more, I would surely have received the word. And so when I heard the news surrounded by my enemies and realised the trap they had set for me, I wept. And when Mountjoy asked me why I wept, I replied that it was for my dearly beloved Queen. A man such as Mountjoy would not have believed me but to tell him the truth openly would have been to sharpen the executioner's blade for my own neck.

However, even if I had received the news, I wonder would it have changed anything? Probably not. I was defeated. Elizabeth's death would have rallied some support for our cause and bought us a little more time but I doubt very much that it would have been enough.

My oath would need to be repeated but to King James VI of Scotland, and soon, England. A Catholic king. Maybe the future was not so grim, after all. We would have to wait to find out.

Chapter LIII
FLIGHT – 1607

As it turned out, I was dealt with leniently by the new King, but I would have received similar terms under Elizabeth. They needed me for the moment to maintain the balance of power in Ulster. I had my anglicised title of the Earl of Tyrone returned to me. I regained control of the majority of my lands. The reparations I was required to pay were paltry considering the length and cost of the war. And I still had control over a great many families. But it is not the same. It is all an act.

And so we are to leave. There is no other way. We are no longer safe in our own country. Rumours are rife that I am to be arrested along with many others any day now. We just cannot go on living in fear from day-to-day. My enemies harass me constantly and my complaints are ignored. When the King came to power I had a feint hope that he might ensure harmony and parity for Catholics. But he is weak.

He allows his sheriffs to do as they wish. They make our lives hell. They steal from us. They intimidate my family. They abuse us verbally and physically. And whom can we go to in order to stop it? Our persecutors and tormentors are the authorities themselves. We cannot raise our voice to them against them, and the King ignores us. When we raise a hand ourselves in defence, the kingdom gasps in horror that the tyrant Tyrone may rebel again. For four years we have endured this. It cannot go on and so we are forced to commit ourselves to exile.

A ship sails from Lough Swilley tomorrow. The O'Neills and the O'Donnells will sail with her. Our ultimate destination is Rome – a beautiful city full of history and mystery. But, alas, it is not home.

THE END

It is four years later as I write this. We came extremely close to driving the strongest empire the world has ever known from our shores. But close is not good enough in a situation like this. It must be all or nothing. We were defeated and in the end there has never been a battle of more significance in Ireland's history than Kinsale.

There is almost a cruel irony to be found in the manner of our defeat: our entire war effort was based on feeding misinformation and rumours to the enemy, while maintaining an excellent and efficient network of communications amongst our forces. How ironic then that our undoing was down to confusion and misinformation on our part and superb communication on the part of the English.

Rumours ran rife after the battle of various informers and traitors – I knew of MacMahon already, so any others were merely token.

However, whether informers sold us with their souls is beside the point. Historians, I am sure, will look back on this episode of Ireland's history and conclude that myriad factors contributed to our ultimate demise and downfall. This is true. But know this – the blame for our defeat lies solely and squarely on the shoulders of one individual and that individual is Hugh O'Neill. I simply was not strong enough when I needed to be to resist the demands of Red and del Aquila. I knew better but I caved in. And the consequences could not be more disastrous.

Ireland is lost forever. And so I fear I will never again set foot in this land. My land. My Ireland.

AFTERMATH

Few episodes in Ireland's colourful history have had effects as far reaching as the Nine Years War and subsequent Flight of the Earls. Even events such as Daniel O'Connell's achievements in the Emancipation movement and Michael Collins's victory in the War of Independence pale in comparison.

It marked the end of Gaelic Ireland because it frightened the English crown into dealing with the situation in the country for once and all. They embarked on the most rigorous plantation campaign in the history of the country. Unlike previous plantations the English aristocracy did not reap the benefits. Instead the Scottish Presbyterian middle and lower classes were employed and their determination to prevail and fight for their new found wealth proved to succeed where all other plantations had failed.

This plantation did not fall victim to its predecessors' frailties such as absentee landlords and lazy attitudes. On the contrary, the beneficiaries of this scheme flourished and went from strength to strength.

The Ulster Plantation laid the foundations for the situation that exists in Northern Ireland to this day.

Printed in the United Kingdom
by Lightning Source UK Ltd.
1807